ANSWER ME

Susanna Tamaro was born in Trieste in 1957 and now lives in Umbria.

ALSO BY SUSANNA TAMARO

Follow Your Heart
For Solo Voice

Susanna Tamaro

ANSWER ME

TRANSLATED BY
Avril Bardoni

VINTAGE

Published by Vintage 2003

2 4 6 8 10 9 7 5 3 1

Copyright © Limmat Stiftung 2001
Translation © Avril Bardoni 2002

Susanna Tamaro has asserted her right under the Copyright,
Designs and Patents Act 1988 to be identified as the author
of this work

First published in Great Britain in 2002 by
Secker & Warburg

Vintage
Random House, 20 Vauxhall Bridge Road,
London SW1V 2SA

Random House Australia (Pty) Limited
20 Alfred Street, Milsons Point, Sydney
New South Wales 2061, Australia

Random House New Zealand Limited
18 Poland Road, Glenfield,
Auckland 10, New Zealand

Random House (Pty) Limited
Endulini, 5A Jubilee Road, Parktown 2193,
South Africa

The Random House Group Limited Reg. No. 954009
www.randomhouse.co.uk

A CIP catalogue record for this book
is available from the British Library

ISBN 0 09 942686 2

Papers used by Random House are natural, recyclable
products made from wood grown in sustainable forests.
The manufacturing processes conform to the environmental regulations of the country of origin

Printed and bound in Denmark by
Nørhaven Paperback A/S, Viborg

Answer Me

Abide in my love.
John 15:9

I

HOW STRANGE TO THINK that it was only last Christmas
that I spent my last holidays with my aunt and uncle. It
was cold and the village lay under a blanket of fog. Life
there was as boring as ever. No one ever phoned, no one
came to see me. My uncle fell asleep in front of the
television while my aunt crocheted voluminous bed-
covers. In the half-darkness the plastic Christmas tree
blinked like defective traffic lights.

Even at midday the fog enveloped the house like a
shroud. Every half-hour I went to the window to look
for a glimmer of sun. I couldn't see a thing. At night I
dreamt that my arms had grown enormously long, long
enough to reach the sky. And when I reached it I pushed
the clouds aside one after the other as if they were heavy
curtains in a cinema. Is the sun here or not? I muttered
angrily. At last I saw it; one gleaming ray fell upon my
forehead. It fell only on me because I was the only one
who had looked for it, forced it out of hiding with my
immeasurably long arms, my persistence.

On New Year's Eve I took myself off to the woodshed
and got drunk. The sound of passing cars reached me

intermittently. Everyone was tearing through the fog. Where were they going? Why did they want to go there? Perhaps they were so miserable they wanted to kill themselves before the festive dinner. The wood smelled of mould and shone wetly like the timbers of a sunken galleon. I'm in the belly of a whale, I thought as everything swam around me. It's swallowed me and I'll never get out again. I'm imprisoned in the dungeons of a castle, or perhaps I'm already dead and this is my grave. My coffin is rotting and my bones are already rotting too. If this is a grave, what about the other side? Surely at some point a crack should appear and I will see the Light of the World. Or flames.

Do I have to believe this? Am I going to fall into this trap again?

Anyway, my mother should be here somewhere. Or perhaps I can't see her because she's already in hell. Or perhaps there's nothing left, nothing at all. After a year we're only worms, after two only dust.

'Say a prayer for Mummy and for the souls in purgatory,' the nuns at the convent told me every evening. I obeyed, kneeling with my hands pressed together, my eyes turned upwards. I expected my mother to appear at any moment, a shaft of light followed by a gust of wind. I would have known it was her from the warmth, the little surge of warmth rising from the pit of my stomach. Love, I would have said to myself, love has made her come back from the realm of the dead.

I prayed and prayed, but the only thing that kept flickering on and off was a faulty light bulb.

Did love really exist? And in what shape or form did it show itself?

The more time passed, the less I understood. It was a word, a word like table, window, lamp. Or was it something else? And how many different kinds of love were there?

As a little girl I believed in it, much as one believes in fairies. But one day I peered into the cracks of bark on the trees, under the lichen. There were neither fairies nor will-o'-the-wisps, only mosses, more lichens, a little earth and a few insects.

The insects weren't kissing, they were eating each other.

My mother died just before I turned eight. In a road accident while I was at school. I remember the day clearly. The teacher took me to the headmistress's room. One laid a hand on my shoulder while the other's lips moved to form the words, 'Something dreadful's happened . . .'

I stood there motionless, dry-eyed. Shall I ever find her scent again, I wondered, and if so, where?

Because faces fade in time, but what about smells? What was her scent, what did it consist of? Cheap cologne certainly, mixed up with the smell of her skin and that of soap or talcum powder. My mother was always washing herself.

For the first seven years of my life we were always together. We lived in a small flat. She was full of fun, outgoing, colourful. After putting me to bed she went off to work, and when I woke up in the morning she was standing beside my bed. She would hurl herself at me, laughing and saying, 'Here's a storm of kisses . . .'

That's how it was, and that's how I expected it to be for ever.

I had not yet learned that our names are not carved in stone but only sketched on a blackboard. Every now and then someone wipes a sponge over it and a name disappears from the list. Do they rub the name out deliberately? For amusement? Had they really meant to rub out that name and not, perhaps, the one just above or just below it?

We had a little picture of Jesus on the door of the kitchenette. There was a little lamp always burning beneath it. Although you couldn't burn your fingers on it, it flickered like a flame. Jesus had his heart in his hand, but that didn't frighten me because, rather than his being dishevelled and screaming with pain, his hair was brushed, his cheeks were pink and he was smiling serenely. 'Who is that man?' I asked the first time I saw him. 'He's a friend,' my mother replied, 'a friend who loves you.' – 'Does he love you too?' – 'Of course. He loves everybody.'

The smell I connect with that day, the day of her death, is of freshly baked bread. There was a bag from the bakery hanging on the back of the headmistress's chair. The smell came from there and filled the room.

On the windowsill a sweet potato was dying slowly in a vase of dirty water.

The 'dreadful thing' was death.

'I want to go to her,' I said.

'I'm sorry, that's no longer possible.'

In the days that followed an almost infinite number of smells superimposed themselves one upon the other. The smell of the hospital, a new and unpleasant smell, the smell of freshly dug earth and flowers already drooping when they arrived, the smell of her friends, Pina, Giulia and Cinzia, all of whom had embraced me many times before, the smell of the surplice worn by the old priest who was in a hurry and gabbled the words, the smell of the mortadella roll one of the bystanders was eating, the smell of the pine dresser in our kitchen.

Now it was she who was shut up in that long, narrow pine dresser.

Her friends cried and blew their noses. The lady looking after me held on to me as if she were afraid I might fly up into the sky.

'Should I cry too?' I asked her. She nodded as if to say 'Yes'. I tried hard, but not very successfully. There was only one thought running through my mind. Where does someone go when they're no longer anywhere?

The next day I began asking Jesus to make me blind. They'd told me at school that he had cured several blind people by spitting on their eyelids. If he did that, I reasoned, he could do the opposite. They say there are some animals who can do this. They spray a liquid into your eyes and you find yourself in a world of darkness.

I wanted this more than anything else. To be in a world where there was nothing, no roads, no houses, no cars, no faces, no morning, no afternoon. Only night. Night in the middle of the ocean, under a cloudy sky, with no stars nor moon nor lights on the horizon.

Blind people usually find their way by feeling. I would have been different, I would have got around by sniffing. I would have detected the smell of red and green traffic lights, that of rain and the stronger smell of a coming snowfall. I would have told nice people from nasty people by their smell, and smell would have told me who to trust and who to bite before they got too close.

I asked Jesus to take me into the dark because I was convinced my mother was hiding there. Searching high and low in the gloom, sooner or later I would have caught a whiff; that whiff would have led me to her, to the tempestuous turbulence of her kisses.

Smell of disinfectant, smell of vegetable soup, of onions,

leeks, smell of unaired rooms, of dust, of dirty skirts, smell of urine in the bedclothes and budget-price soap, smell of damp, smell of incense. Among all these smells I couldn't find one I recognised as mine.

At the convent where I boarded there was one nun who always put her arms around me. She was trying to comfort me, but instead she frightened me.

I was still not blind, but I had learned to play a trick with my eyes nevertheless. When someone stood in front of me I imagined myself to be a snail and waved them forwards and backwards, backwards and forwards until everything went misty.

Only the evening brought me peace, when we knelt beside our beds in our pyjamas and the sister said, 'Let's put our little hands together and pray to Jesus.'

Jesus had followed me from my previous existence to this one and, as he was my friend and loved me, was something good. So, with my hands pressed together I would repeat silently, 'Please, seeing that you love me and love my mummy too, bring us together again for ever.'

The Jesus of the dormitory, however, was different from the Jesus of the kitchenette. Instead of holding his heart in his hand and smiling, he was nailed to a cross, dirty, semi-naked, his eyes shut. He hung there in his pain and looked at nobody.

Meanwhile, they were trying to find my relatives. I'd never had a father. My mother had no brothers or sisters. Her parents had been dead for a long time.

'You are lucky,' the girl in the bed next to mine said one day. 'They'll have to have you adopted.'

So as the weeks stretched into months that too became my dream. I had no wish for another mother, but I would have liked to have a father at last and a home with a room of my own for my own games, my own smells.

One day a social worker arrived. She had red cheeks and was wearing a very shabby bottle-green overcoat. 'What a lucky girl you are!' she exclaimed gaily. 'Today we're going to pack your case and tomorrow you're going to your aunt and uncle. Uncle Luciano is your grandfather's brother. He has a wife but no children. During the Christmas and summer holidays you'll be living with them in the country. Are you pleased?'

I didn't say yes or no. I stood there with my snail-eyes going backwards and forwards.

My uncle came to fetch me the next day. His shoes squeaked as he crossed the wide hall. Instead of kissing me he held out his hand and said, 'How do you do? I'm Luciano.'

His car had very shiny red plastic seats. In the back were two round cushions with crocheted covers that were a mass of frills and flounces. Every time we went round a corner they shook like two great jellyfish. We hardly spoke a word.

'Now you will meet your Aunt Elide,' he said just before we arrived.

My aunt looked as if she had been carved out of wood. Hard red cheeks and a very large nose. She gave me two kisses that felt like bites and said, 'Welcome.'

That afternoon I helped her to clean out the hen house. The next day we prepared the biscuits for Christmas. She hardly uttered a word. 'Give me this, take that.'

I had a room upstairs with a big cold bed. There was a small table, a wardrobe and a tiled floor. From the window you could see the flyover above the main road. *Vuoom, vuoom* went the cars. *Grrrrn* went the trucks.

Fogs were frequent. In those days the big artics looked like mammoths. They appeared out of nowhere, like phantoms, and into nowhere they vanished again.

That Christmas I found a parcel under the artificial Christmas tree with its flashing lights. Inside was a box. In the box was a white blouse.

'Do you like it?' asked Aunt Elide.

'Yes,' I replied.

In point of fact I cared nothing for the blouse. The one thing I really wanted was a teddy bear to share my bed. The one I had had all my life had disappeared into the world of darkness with everything else.

I was given a white blouse that Christmas and for nearly every Christmas afterwards. Each one more buttoned-up, more chaste than the last.

II

At the convent I was always on my own. Every so often a sister would draw me aside and say, 'It's not good to isolate yourself from other people. It will only make you sad.' So to please her I would rejoin my classmates and stand in the circle, but no one ever threw the ball to me. I stayed for a while, doing nothing, then returned to my bench and my thoughts.

Thoughts can be good or bad, the nuns often used to say. Which were the good ones and which the bad? How could you tell one kind from the other? Thoughts have no smell, and this makes everything more difficult.

I wandered up and down the garden paths and thought. I reckoned that if God had really cared about us, he would have given thoughts a perfume, too, so that you could tell what kind they were from the moment they formed in your mind. To be close to a rose is quite different from being close to a primula. The former knocks you over with its scent, the latter you hardly notice. In the same way, bad thoughts ought to have a bad smell, a disgusting smell like manure or rotting fish, for example, and good thoughts should have a gentle, pleasant perfume, an aroma like vanilla or chocolate. This would make the world a much simpler place. Nobody could hide behind words because everyone would notice the stench or the fragrant perfume at once. Anyone with bad thoughts or evil intentions would be rumbled even before they opened their mouth.

It was when I was about eight and attending catechism classes that I learnt about the existence of guardian angels. Ever afterwards, when anyone asked me why I was always alone, I would answer, 'I'm not alone, I've got my guardian angel with me.'

'Rosa's angel is always with her,' the nuns would whisper, watching me from a distance. The elderly one who opened the door for visitors would murmur, 'God bless you,' as she passed me. So they left me to it and I could think my thoughts in peace.

One thing had me worried for some time. It was about Jesus. I had been making a few calculations. There were twelve of us in the dormitory and every evening each of us had some request for him. Besides ours, there were four more dormitories whose occupants also made similar requests and then there were the nuns as well. All in all, he had quite a few people to attend to just within our little community. If one then considered all the people outside the convent as well, the numbers grew to a terrifying total. How could Jesus even remember all these requests, and above all, how could he possibly grant them? And then, were we absolutely certain that he did grant them? My mother had told me that Jesus loved me and that he loved her too. The nuns said he loved everyone.

But what was love? That was something I couldn't understand. It was not a smell nor a coin you could buy things with. The nuns spoke of love as if it were a glue holding the world together, but they put blinds on the windows and read our letters for fear that love might explode like a bomb in our midst. What kind of love were they talking about?

The more I thought about it the less I understood. I asked the girl sitting next to me in class. 'It's when a man and a woman sleep together with no clothes on, one on top of the other.'

Summers with my uncle and aunt seemed interminable. No one ever came to visit. We never went on trips except on August bank-holiday to a nearby shrine in honour of Mary. There was no breath of wind, the light was dazzling, the excrement lying about fermented in the heat. Rabbit-piddle, chicken-turds. You couldn't go outside the house without holding your nose.

'You'll just have to get used to it, my fine young lady,' sneered my aunt. I knew what was in her mind: that one day the chickens, the rabbits, the woodshed and the house with its kitchen garden and fruit trees would be mine. I had to get used to it because this was how I would spend the rest of my life, cleaning out chickens, wringing their necks, picking, peeling and boiling tomatoes, skinning rabbits and then, in the evening, exhausted, sitting outside the house at sunset and watching the trucks belting along the highway.

'If it wasn't for us . . .' she said over and over again.

If it wasn't for you, I thought to myself, by now I would have a good home and a father. Or perhaps I'd be at the seaside with the nuns and my classmates. Still, it's so much better to be here, inhaling exhaust fumes from the trucks and methane from decomposing turds.

People, too, smelt more in summer. At a distance of thirty metres and with my eyes shut I could tell my aunt from my uncle, the parish priest from the postman.

Noises became almost overwhelming in the heat. *Vrooom vroooom* went the heavy diesel trucks on the flyover. *Bzzzzbzz* went the flies. *Croak croak* went the frogs in a nearby ditch. And then, at night, the mosquitoes. Mosquitoes of all shapes and sizes. As soon as you turned the light off, they homed in on you, whining around your ears, *zssszss*. Killing them was useless. For every one you killed, ten more materialised.

In the kitchen, my uncle had installed a kind of lamp he'd bought at a fair. As soon as an insect touched it, it was burnt to a crisp. It made a sound like *chics*, and smelt like burnt chicken. Every time an insect died, my aunt cried, 'There goes another one!' and recited the day's score.

Zsss, croak, vroomm, chics, bzzzzbzz . . . Who was there to talk to? All the questions that had been piling up in my head through the winter became a tight band around it in the summer.

My aunt disliked me, my uncle ignored me. The postman always gave me a sweet and the priest couldn't stand the sight of me.

I realised this the first time I saw him. He smelt of chicken soup, of wine-cellar, of something unclean whatever it was. He had small slitty eyes like a wild boar. When my aunt introduced me to him he stood there looking at me as if I were a kind of insect. He didn't shake my hand or offer any caress. He just tapped the side of his nose and said, 'Ah yes, Marisa's daughter.'

Despite this, I went to see him one day in August. If Don Firmato couldn't answer my questions, who could? I found him dozing in the cool darkness at the back of the church. Sitting down beside him, I gently touched his sleeve.

'Oh it's you,' he stammered.

'There's something I need to know.'

'Tell me.'

'What is love?'

He turned to look at me, his eyes slow-moving, watery.

'How old are you?'

'Twelve.'

'Love is sin.'

Of all the sins, Don Firmato's favourites were the sins of the flesh; because of this the children nicknamed him Don Bistecca, Don Beefsteak. Not a Sunday passed but, after taking a longer or a shorter route, he would finally get round to this subject. Even if the reading for the day was the Beatitudes, he still managed to preach that the path to perdition lay through the senses. Don Firmato's world was divided into two by a wall so high no one could climb over it. Some were on this side and some on that. On one side lay heaven, on the other hell. A person's destiny was decided at birth. There was no possibility of choice. Everything was decided from the start.

One day someone wrote 'Firmato = Pig' in red paint on the walls of the presbytery. When I saw it, I couldn't help laughing.

That same afternoon the carabinieri came to the house to question my aunt at some length. Was the house door left unlocked at night or not? Was it possible to leave the house through a window and get in again without anyone noticing? Then they went up to my bedroom and looked in the wardrobe and under the bed. They checked my hands and wrists. They even examined my nails for traces of red paint.

Standing behind them, my aunt kept saying, 'My niece is a good girl. She comes to Mass with me every Sunday. She goes to bed early. And apart from that, if it was her I would kill her with my bare hands.'

The carabinieri nodded solemnly. Don Firmato must have been absolutely convinced of my guilt. If it had been up to him, I'd have been burning in hellfire already. The only reason my aunt defended me was because she knew it was impossible for me to get out of the house at night. Every evening, in fact, she locked all the doors, and from the second storey, where I slept, there was no way of getting down to the ground without breaking a leg.

All the same, the next day I had to join the little group of the faithful charged with cleaning the presbytery wall. Passing close by me, Don Firmato hissed, 'Like mother, like daughter. She is in hell and you are already in the antechamber.'

My mother was a prostitute. At eight years old I knew nothing of this; I thought her work was cleaning offices at night. I believed this until I was eleven.

Meanwhile, dreams of following her into the darkness had vanished. The nuns had called in a psychiatrist to help me. The psychiatrist came to the convent; we spoke in a room, just the two of us.

'Death,' he said. 'Can you understand what death means? It means that your mother no longer walks upon this earth, that you will never again be able to open a door and see her. Never again will you be able to touch her or put your arms round her. You must come to terms with the idea of living with lovely memories of her.' Then he touched my arm lightly with the tips of his fingers and said, 'If you feel like crying, cry.'

Everyone wanted me to cry, except me. Instead of crying, I asked myself: what happens to the rubbish? Rubbish is like this, too. One day there's a plastic bag in the corner under the sink, and the next day it's gone. A big truck comes along and swallows it up. When the truck's gone, all that's left is a nasty smell in the air.

Death cannot be so very different; it too went around and swallowed people up as if they were plastic bags, leaving behind a stinking cloud. The same smell as when a dog got run over by a truck on the highway.

I learned the truth when it was shouted in my face by Aunt Elide one morning. She was cross with me about something. When this happened her eyes went as hard as glass, her tongue cut like a knife. 'It's time to stop the pretence,' she shouted. Then she dragged out the truth like passing the beads of a rosary through her fingers. 'Your mother did not die in a car crash, but was hit by a car while waiting for her clients on a street corner.'

'What was she selling?' I asked.

My aunt looked at me hard, with sneering defiance. 'Don't you understand? She was selling her body. The only thing that woman was capable of doing was opening her legs.'

From that day on, every time she spoke about her, Aunt Elide referred to her with those words. The woman who opened her legs.

I put up with this for over a year. Then one morning in the kitchen, as soon as she started to say, 'The only thing that woman . . .' I flared up.

'She was also capable of opening her arms!' I yelled. Aunt Elide's face went white.

'Wicked girl,' she hissed. 'After all the sacrifices we make for you.'

I seized the tongs, picked up a glowing coal from the fireplace and waved it about close to the curtains.

'Touch me and I'll set fire to the house.'

My uncle hurried to her assistance. 'Water puts out fire,' he said, and threw a jug of water over me.

Was that the day I began to hate them?

I believe it was.

I stayed in my bedroom writing little notes. I hate you, I hope you die, I hope you get run over by a car, that you have a stroke, some awful disease. I decorated the notes with little drawings, then I tore them all up into tiny pieces, went to the bathroom and before flushing them down the pan did my business on top of them.

In their presence, however, I allowed nothing to show but forced myself to be all sweetness and light. I was afraid of reprisals. My uncle was always threatening to lock me in the woodshed because it was alive with mice, spiders and snakes. To conquer my fear of it, I began to go there by myself. Once in there, no one could find me and no one bothered me. Within a short time the woodshed became my favourite place of refuge. By then, human beings frightened me more than mice and snakes.

Once, when I was cycling along a dusty white road, I met a woman with two children in tow, yelling like mad because there was a grass snake a few feet away. To show her they were harmless, I got off my bike, seized it by the tail and shoved it under her nose. 'Look,' I said, 'you only have to hold it by the tail. There's no way it can turn itself round.' Instead of thanking me, she continued to howl like one obsessed.

Next day the whole village was saying that there was something funny about me because I kept snakes in my pocket and stroked their noses as if they were dogs.

III

At thirteen I'd had more than enough of my aunt and uncle. The mere thought of their voices and faces was enough to make me squirm. So a few days before Christmas I decided that I was not going to them. I asked to speak to Mother Superior and told her.

'Why?' she asked, looking me straight in the eyes.

'Because I don't like it there.'

'Is anything wrong?'

'No. They're old and I get bored. That's all.'

'Then I'm sorry, but you'll have to go. The court made them your guardians. Besides, spending Christmas alone is worse than being alone any other time of year. If you stayed here, you'd soon come to regret it.'

All through the night I mulled over the idea of running away, but in the morning I did the same as I'd done all the other years. I got on the coach and went to the farm.

The biscuits were already in the oven.

'Here you are at last!' exclaimed my aunt as I opened the door. 'Get changed and clean out the rabbits. Then come back here, because the capon still has to be plucked.'

I worked for her throughout the day before Christmas Eve.

In the evening a freezing drizzle began to fall. We ate in silence at the Formica-topped kitchen table, in front of the television which was on. The windows were all steamed up. The turkey was boiling in a big pot, but because the bird was too big for the pot, the stumps of its legs stuck out at the top.

I washed up and went to bed. The sheets were freezing and the coverlet felt damp. *Vroom grnn vroom.* Although the window was shut, I could still hear the sound of the cars and lorries. A prayer rose to my lips out of habit, but I sent it back whence it came. I was too old now for teddy bears but hadn't yet managed to get a handle on prayers. Was there an antidote to sorrow? I wanted to cry but my eyes remained obstinately dry. My body felt as though it belonged to someone else. I tried to cuddle myself. Cold on cold. Like two snakes cuddling or two bits of metal. Now I'm going to jump out of the window, I thought. I probably won't kill myself but I might at least break my legs or my back, then I'll spend Christmas in hospital and the rest of my life in a wheelchair. At that precise moment I seemed to smell my mother's scent. I switched on the light. There was no one in the room. Where did it come from? Did I really smell it or was it just a dream? On the ceiling, right over my bed, a patch of mould had appeared. It had the shape of a bear's head or the head of an ape with its mouth open.

The sound of the television still came from downstairs. The two monoliths were there, sitting on the armchairs draped with plastic dustsheets. Two dried-up insects. Two mummies with skin like wrinkled parchment. My aunt gave the orders, my uncle obeyed. 'Yes, Elide. Very well, Elide. You're quite right, Elide.'

Throughout Christmas Eve I tried to keep calm. As soon as my aunt told me to do something, I obeyed. I kept my eyes on the ground the whole time so that she shouldn't read my mind. Every now and then I went up to my room and hurled the pillow fiercely against the wall, then buried my head in it and howled silently.

In the evening we were due to open our presents, exchange thankyou kisses, eat slices of cold turkey while watching some variety show with my uncle laughing at the stupidest, the most vulgar jokes.

I was prepared for the sixth white blouse, but received a pair of blue wool gloves trimmed with fake leather instead. I had a surprise for my uncle and aunt, too. Instead of the usual pottery flower-vase made by myself at school or crocheted oven-gloves, I gave them a pear and an apple tied with a big red bow. Year after year, casting aside the presents she received, my aunt had exclaimed, 'How nice it used to be at Christmas when our only presents were a couple of walnuts and an orange!' Now, thanks to me, she had her wish.

Then we sat down to dinner. Just as my aunt was lamenting that her tortellini weren't as successful as last year's and my uncle was reassuring her by saying he thought they were actually even better, the doorbell rang. My aunt stretched her neck like a turkey.

'Who can it be at this time of night? And today of all days?'

I got up and went to open the door. There stood a black man with a big bag. He was selling knickers and hand-towels. The whites of his eyes gleamed in the darkness.

'Would you like to buy something nice?' he asked.

'Come in,' I said. 'We're having Christmas dinner.'

My aunt sprang to her feet. 'Who is it?' she shrieked. 'What d'you think you're doing letting strangers in?'

'Is this Christmas dinner or isn't it?' I rejoined.

'Not for him it isn't. If he were a Christian he would certainly not be going from door to door selling his bits and bobs of rags this evening of all evenings.'

My uncle had got up from the table and now, falteringly, touched the black man's hand.

'Thank you,' he said, asserting his authority as a man, 'but we don't need anything.' And he showed him to the door.

'Did you lock it properly?' asked my aunt when he returned.

'Indeed I did.'

We continued to eat in silence. There were children of every colour on the television, got up like chimpanzees in a circus, singing fatuous little Christmas ditties while adults stood around and applauded, their eyes glistening.

I banged my spoon on the edge of my plate.

The monoliths raised their heads.

'Supposing that had been Jesus?' I said.

Aunt Elide got up to collect the plates. 'Don't be silly. Jesus wasn't a black man. Nor did he go from door to door selling knickers.'

When the dish of boiled turkey was passed to me, I thought it looked like slices from a corpse, as indeed it was, and refused it.

'How do you know you don't like it if you don't even taste it?'

Instead of telling her to go to hell, I simply said, 'I've lost my appetite.'

She speared a slice with her fork and slapped it on to my plate. 'You'll eat it all the same.'

At that point something strange happened. My heart felt as if it were beginning to swell. It was as if someone had unscrewed an artery and attached a bicycle pump in its place. The manometer rose and my heart got bigger and bigger. What would happen if it started to push against the sharp bones of my ribs?

So I opened my mouth.

'Why don't we talk about love?'

'About what love?' snapped Turkey-Neck.

'I don't know. I'm asking you. How many loves are there? Two? Three? Four? Ten? A thousand? Seeing that you're married, you ought to know at least one, shouldn't you? Or perhaps you . . .'

My uncle stood up. He was trembling all over.

'Show some respect, or . . .!'

'I was only asking! I don't know what love is, where it is. I don't even know if it exists and how . . .'

My aunt interrupted me with a little smile:

'You should have asked your mother. She was a specialist.'

At that moment my heart touched my ribs and threw everything out of place. I picked up the slice of turkey in my fingers, threw it on the floor and stamped on it. 'I hate meat!' I screamed. 'I hate it!' And I went out, slamming the door behind me.

It was cold outside and I hadn't put on my jacket. Aunt Elide's bicycle was propped against the wall; I got on it and began to pedal. I had no idea where I was going, but only felt an incredible strength in my legs.

The sky had a few clouds and a few stars in it.

The wheel of the dynamo went *vrrrr* against the rim of the cycle wheel, creating a light that was too dim and intermittent to make much impression on the darkness of the night.

Almost without noticing it, I arrived at the station. It was shortly before ten o'clock and the little buffet was still open. I went in and said, 'A grappa.'

It was the first time in my life that I had ordered anything except hot chocolate.

The first sip made me cough, as did the second. After the third I felt my legs going wobbly. I saw the lights of a pinball machine in a corner.

'When's the next train?' I asked.

'The last one's already gone,' replied the man behind the counter, polishing the glasses. 'And there won't be another until tomorrow morning.'

He had a broad face with a thick, drooping moustache. He might be my father, I thought. Like me, my mother had come to the station, running away from something or other and frightened; she had sat silently in a corner and he, pretending to comfort her, had pinned her against the toilet wall with his big, heavy body. And nine months later I was born.

I had finished my drink and was feeling peculiar.

'Have you got any children?' I asked stupidly.

'No, unfortunately,' he replied. 'All the same, I know it's not right for you to be hanging round here at this time of night. Now I'm going to close the bar and you're going home, agreed?'

He accompanied me outside and pulled down the shutter. He had a decrepit Fiat 127 which took a bit of coaxing before the engine got going. At every attempt, the silencer shook so violently it seemed about to fall off. Then he drove away leaving a wake of big white clouds.

Should I go back home? What awaited me at home? Suppose I went back to the convent instead? Perhaps there was no one left there either, as all the nuns would have gone to visit their families. After the episode with the live coal I had never dared rebel against my aunt and uncle in that way again. At most, I had been a bit offhand. How would they greet me? I had, after all, been an unwelcome guest from the outset.

Looking up, I saw a satellite crossing the sky. It looked like the Star of Bethlehem. It was Christmas night. Perhaps my fears were groundless. Perhaps the comet with its fiery tail had warmed even the hearts of my aunt and uncle. I could knock on the door and, for the first time ever, they would welcome me with open arms.

I was already riding homewards when I heard someone call me. It was the knicker-salesman. He was sitting surrounded by his bags of merchandise, smoking.

'You're here,' I said.

He gestured to me to sit beside him and held out his cigarette. One, two, three puffs. At the third puff, something grabbed my stomach and turned it upside down. Where was I? Was I in a boat? I felt sick, as if I were being tossed about on a rough sea. Everything swam around me. Yes, I was in a boat and the boat was sinking, it was being spun around by a whirlpool and was about to carry me to the bottom. 'First cigarette?' asked the black man. He rested his hand on my leg, at the top near the groin.

Suddenly the whirlpool stopped spinning and I burst out laughing. The night was black, the road was black, the knicker-seller was black. What colour was the soul? Perhaps it too was black, which was why it had always escaped me. Instead of sinking, I was now staggering, holding my arms out in front of me like a child playing blindman's buff. Where was the edge of anything? I could no longer find it.

A train passed along the rails behind us. The noise drowned out his words. What was that smell? A smell of woods, of jungle, the smell of hunted and hunting animals. His body was very close to mine, so close he was squashing me. Did he want to warm me up? Then why was he pressing so hard? I no longer felt like laughing, but more like crying. I saw the whites of his eyes, his hands were invisible in the darkness. How many hands did he have? I seemed to feel them all over me. When a sort of powerful slug entered my mouth, I snapped my teeth shut in self-defence.

All of a sudden I found myself on the ground. He was shouting incomprehensibly and spitting. Then I felt a kick in the back.

Immediately I was on the bike and pedalling hard.

I pedalled and pedalled through the night with the lamp out, and felt as if I were not moving at all. My legs were as heavy as in a nightmare, when you have to escape but nothing responds to your commands. At first I was wet with perspiration. Then the perspiration turned to ice. A motorist, overtaking me at speed, sounded his horn at me angrily. I nearly lost my balance. When I put my feet on the ground again I looked around and saw nothing I recognised. Not a single hoarding, traffic light, farm building.

Where was I going? And who was I? I looked at the fingers gripping the brakes as if they belonged to a stranger. What was my name? It was like trying to catch a fish with my hands; the more I tried, the more it slipped away. There was no one around to ask, 'Do you know who I am?'

Suddenly an enormous cavity opened inside me, and inside that cavity I circled with eyes and mouth both wide open, like a goldfish in a bowl. I was both the fish and its owner. I existed and I watched myself existing. And yet, although I existed and was watching myself existing, I was not certain that I existed at all.

Then unexpectedly and all together, the church bells began to ring. I woke up. It's Christmas, I said, and I'm Rosa. The Rosa who stormed out of the house with bits of turkey stuck to her shoes, the Rosa nobody wants, the Rosa all thorns and no flowers, the Rosa who's just been kicked by a black man. I looked around and understood where I was at last, so I started pedalling once more towards the village.

If I had not smoked that cigarette would everything have turned out differently? Who knows. The grappa was in my stomach, the first grappa of my life. The smoke of the cigarette turned it into dynamite.

I rode not calmly but furiously. The lamp had gone out again, but the dynamo still whirred round, no longer charging light but the darkness of my heart. At every turn of the chain, confused sadness and a vague sense of humiliation transformed themselves into hate. A pure hate, as transparent and indestructible as carbon in a diamond. Rising into my mouth, the hate became vocal. Dashing along the road I shouted, 'Go to hell, all of you! Die, you turds, you shitty bastards!'

My heart was now well against my ribs, entangled in them like a balloon in the branches of a tree. The smallest of movements would have made it burst. My ribs were like knives. As I breathed, they dug into the flesh. The deeper I breathed, the sharper the pain became. Perhaps an abscess had formed on a ventricle and was about to burst.

The space in front of the church was crammed with cars. Warm candlelight filtered through the windows. I slung my bicycle to the ground. Had anyone been standing in front of the door I would have punched them. There was no one, so I kicked the door open.

Everything then happened very quickly. The church was full. Although the sermon was in full swing, everyone turned round to look at me. I covered the length of the nave with great strides.

'You all make me sick!' I yelled. 'And d'you know why? Because you're nothing but foul, disgusting whited sepulchres!'

The priest stood there with his mouth open and one arm suspended in mid-air. Some of the children started to laugh. I went to the manger-scene, snatched the baby from the manger and held it over my head like a football trophy.

'Do you know what this is?' I shouted, spinning it in the air. 'Do you know what this really is? It's a stupid little doll!'

The noise of the baby smashing into splinters roused them. They all crossed themselves. I saw my aunt flop down in the front row, my uncle leap out of the pew to catch me.

Don Firmato grabbed a candlestick and lurched towards me.

I escaped by ducking down the left-hand aisle. As I dashed past, I tore the coloured posters announcing the catechism from their place. In big letters was written: 'Love is . . .' I tossed them on to the candles burning before the statue of St Anthony. They flared up in less than a second. I was already by the door.

Before I left, I turned and shouted with all the breath in my lungs.

'Hear this, Pig Firmato! Love means kissing Our Lady, not puking in her face!'

Then I leapt on the bike and went home.

Did I want to die? Probably. The house was empty. Coals still smoked on the floor of the hearth.

Suddenly, I didn't know what to do next. I felt drained. My heart was no longer thumping, but my head was. There was an agonising pain behind my eyes. Everything was spinning around me. I collapsed on to the plastic-covered armchair. What would happen next? Would the carabinieri come to arrest me? Perhaps my aunt would kill me. What was it she said to the maresciallo the other day? 'With my bare hands.'

I was too tired to feel fear of any kind. Nothing was

going right so everything was going right. Not far away a dog began to howl miserably. From the road came the sound of cars on their way home.

'Mamma . . .' I murmured before drifting off to sleep and, while sleeping only a matter of minutes, dreamed of her embrace. She held me tightly, smiling, saying nothing. Then suddenly my aunt was standing over me, shouting and brandishing the fire-tongs. When the tongs hit me I realised the dream was over. I no longer wanted to die, so I tried to slide off the armchair.

'Don't let her get away, grab her!' she shouted at my uncle. He hurled himself at me in a rugby tackle. We slid, both at full-length on the floor, out into the passage.

'I'll kill you! I'll kill you, bastard spawn of Satan!' my aunt shrieked over and over again. And continued to hit me. She hit me as she beat the blankets, in a blind fury. I tried to protect my head with my arms. When I saw the blood, I too started to shout.

'Kill me, then! Go on, kill me! Then there'll be nothing to stop me taking you to hell with me!'

She hit me another couple of times, the blows getting weaker each time, then threw the tongs to the floor, put her hands over her face and burst into sobs.

The neighbours' dog was still barking.

I stayed in bed for two days. I didn't want to eat, I didn't want anything. Even the effort of moving a leg was too much. Some of the time I slept, some of the time I spent looking at the patches of mould on the ceiling.

On the afternoon of the second day I heard the maresciallo's voice in the kitchen. He hadn't come to take me away, as I hoped, but only to say that Don Firmato, out of respect for my aunt's piety and her diligent attendance at the Mass, had withdrawn all charges. 'Indeed,' he added, 'everyone in the village is thinking of you.'

Aunt Elide thanked him in a voice the shadow of its usual self. 'And to think I took her in out of pure charity. Fatherless, and the child of that woman! And we are getting old. We hoped to be the means of her salvation. You understand me. And now we have this cross to carry.'

Before he left, the maresciallo said, 'You must be brave.'

On the third day, when my aunt and uncle had gone into town, I went downstairs, found the bottle of alkermes used for flavouring sweetmeats and hid with it in the woodshed.

IV

How many layers of skin do we have on our bodies? You can get first-, second- or third-degree abrasions. There's the minor abrasion you get when you knock against something, and there's the one when the skin is literally peeled off. There's the same difference between those extremes as there is between a slight annoyance and a threat to life. Skin helps us to breathe and protects the more delicate layers of tissue.

How many layers were left on me?

Sitting on the saw-horse I drank the alkermes and studied my arm. There was still skin in some places but not in others. The pain should have been limited to certain areas, but on the contrary its tentacles reached everywhere. Perhaps my face, too, was skinned. No longer pink but bright scarlet, like the face of an ape from Borneo. Or that of the Devil.

Was there really such a place as hell? If there was nothing above us, was there also nothing beneath our feet? Or rather, was there some gross imbalance between the two extremes? Above, a gleaming sky as insubstantial as a veil of gossamer, and, down below, all the leftovers, the detritus of the world? Perhaps that was why the world remained in one piece, because the centre was so extraordinarily heavy.

There must be fire down there, and lead and tin and coal. And all the blackest souls besides. They wallow in the flames like pigs in mud. Without this heavy core our planet would be like a meringue: voluminous but light as a feather. Straying from its proper course, it would explode like a snowball against a car windscreen. So as it is still in one piece, the centre must be heavy. Heavy and inhabited, like an apple with a grub inside it.

Every house has a landlord. What did the landlord of hell look like? Was his the face that loomed over our own lives?

When I had torn up the poster displaying the words 'Love is . . .' and held it to the flames, it had caught fire immediately. It could have put up some sort of resistance, fought for a few minutes before allowing itself to be reduced to ashes. Then people could have said, 'You see? Love is proof against fire. Or at least it tries to be . . .'

Love conquers everything, I had frequently been told. Love is stronger than death. But that wasn't true, because love, even if it exists, is flimsy, insubstantial, so insubstantial that it is nearly invisible. And to be invisible and to be non-existent are practically the same thing. Smoke from a heath-fire can be seen from far away, and for years afterwards the fire-damage can be seen all around. But you cannot see love even if it's right in front of you.

I too was burning. My body was burning and I was burning inside. That was why I drank, hoping for some kind of relief. But the relief was short-lived. I would have had to roll in frozen snow or shout in a voice of thunder all that was in my heart.

'Hate' was my favourite word. I began to whisper it to myself over and over again. I hate you. I hate you both. I hate myself. I hate you. I hate you both. I hate myself. Then I left out the pronouns and all that remained was 'hate'. *Odio*. Separating the letters, I transformed it into *O Dio* . . . Oh God! . . .

Why was everyone so afraid of ending up in hell? I found the thought of ending up in heaven much more frightening. I could have looked the Devil squarely in the face, but not God! Absolutely impossible. He would have seen my paltriness. He would have despised me as I despised the priest and my aunt. Besides, I had broken the statue of the Child Jesus. I had broken it on the holiest night, the night of his birth. Where could I ever hope to end up, if it was true that there was life after death?

That night, lying in bed, I thought that if it was possible to pray to an angel, then it must also be possible to pray to the Devil. I experimented by reciting a prayer to the Angel of God and substituting the name of the Devil for that of the Angel. Afterwards, however, I found I couldn't sleep. The patch on the ceiling seemed to have developed a thousand eyes, fluorescent eyes and tongues that shot shafts of lightning through the dark room. I was woken up in the middle of the night by the sound of my own voice screaming. For a second I thought that the patch on the ceiling was a great ape with blood smeared around its mouth and eyes that shone like red-hot coals, and that it was hurling itself at me.

I spent the rest of the holiday like a stowaway on board ship. I shut myself in my room. As soon as I heard them go out I went downstairs to the kitchen.

29

On the fourth of January I decided to return to school. I told my aunt while she was feeding the chickens. She said neither yes nor no nor anything else. She didn't even look up from the pail of chicken-feed.

I packed my few belongings in a bag. The bus left at midday. My uncle was out hunting. When my aunt left to go to market I mixed rat poison with the feed for the chickens and rabbits.

'You're back early!' remarked Mother Superior when she saw me.

We went into her study. Steam was coming out of an electric kettle. She turned the kettle off, poured the boiling water into a teapot and sat down in front of me.

'Has something happened?' she asked.

I shrugged my shoulders. 'Absolutely nothing. I was bored.'

The insistent way she looked at me made me feel uneasy.

'What happened to your face?'

'I fell off my bicycle.'

The clock behind the desk chimed half past four. Outside it was almost dark. Mother Superior's hand touched mine. Her voice was soft and gentle.

'Rosa, why don't you tell the truth? You have nothing to fear from me.'

'There's no such thing as truth.'

'Are you sure?'

I blurted out the first thing that came into my head. 'Nobody loves me. Nobody cares if I live or die.'

'You're wrong. I care about you.'

'You only care about the fees.'

'What can I do to convince you otherwise?'

'Nothing.'

'Would you like me to send for the psychologist?'

'I detest psychologists.'

'Then what?'

'Things are all right as they are.'

'I don't think they are all right.'

'They're all right as far as I'm concerned, and there's no more to be said.'

At that point I felt her hands on mine. They were small and rather cold.

'Why don't you look me in the eyes?'

'I don't have to.'

'You don't have to, but it would be good manners.'

'I don't give a fig for good manners.'

At that moment the bell sounded for evening prayers. Mother Superior got up.

'I have to go, but before you leave there are two things I want to say. The first is this, that the doors to my study and my room are never locked, day or night, and if you want to speak to me you only have to turn the handle and come in . . .'

'And the second?'

'Remember that you have no responsibility for your past but a great deal for your future. Your future is in your hands and it is you who must shape it. That is why I am asking you to reflect and talk things over before doing anything you might regret.'

The months that followed were months of darkness, shot through with sudden and extremely violent shafts of light. Everything seemed futile, company of any kind was unbearable. I attended lessons but heard nothing of what the teachers said. I spent hours poring over my books but the pages might as well have been blank. I only had a year left before leaving school, but the prospect did nothing to raise my spirits.

My future stretched before me as blank as the pages.

I was apparently fated to return to the farm and spend the rest of my days cleaning up rabbit and chicken droppings. The day would come when my aunt and uncle would both be dead and I would own everything, but it would be too late. Old and ugly, I would find no one with whom to share my life. Or perhaps I would let everything go and take to living on the streets with the stray dogs. They, at least, would love me. Maybe none of this would happen. I would simply stay at the farm and, as the years rolled by, the fog would seep into my gut and consume my bones. Alcohol would already have consumed my brain. Between my nose and ears there would be a darkness as black as a ship's hold, and inside it a single idea, as old as the hills, would be churning: the problem of finding the easiest way to end it all. So, one day, I would drag myself, tottering, to the woodshed and hang myself from the highest beam. The local papers would give it a short mention on an inside page: *Disturbed woman found dead at home.*

Meanwhile, my classmates could speak of nothing but their hopes for the future. Some dreamt of marriage, some of going to university. One wanted to be a nurse, another a forestry worker. The shyest and quietest girl of all wanted, it was rumoured, to stay in the convent as a cloistered nun for the rest of her life. I kept my thoughts to myself. If someone started asking questions, I gave the most banal of answers. I'm going to work with computers; I shall help my aunt and uncle on the farm.

Sometimes, in the middle of the ocean, an island appears that was never there before, or lava from a volcano wipes out or creates a whole region. Something along those lines was happening to me, but what was being created inside me was no island, rather a bog. It was a bog where there was neither dawn nor sunset, where no winds rustled through the grasses or the boughs of willow. The air was dark and still. In this dark, still air the mud exuded noxious gases. At night I smelt them oozing slowly from every orifice of my body. It was a smell of methane, sulphur, of something decaying in the depths.

Winter passed and the days began to lengthen. Swallows and blackbirds flitted busily from one part of the garden to another and the buds began to swell on the boughs. Among the grasses lining the ditches and hillsides the first flowers began to appear, purple violets and pale yellow primroses. Touched by the rays of the sun, everything started to return to life. With the change of season, even the fermentation in the bog began to produce a kind of energy. Had the same not happened to the first organisms when the world began? In those pools without oxygen the amino-acids had, at a specific moment, become hyperactive, giving rise to life. This activity was not self-induced but came about with the help of a flash of lightning that, hitting the water, produced a short-circuit. Inside me, too, flashes of lighting were beginning to strike, whistling and exploding like fireworks on New Year's Eve, their brightness momentarily tearing aside the veil of darkness. Walking down the long corridors, I wondered for how much longer I could keep this tremendous energy hidden.

The short-circuit happened at Easter, during the Mass. While the offertory was in progress, suddenly the shafts of lightning deserted their usual trajectory and instead of being quenched in the muddy water aimed themselves at my head. In a split second I saw everything and was blinded, heard everything and was deafened. There was power, energy, devastation inside me. I ran to the wall and started hitting my head against it. Which would last out longer, my head or the wall? In some way I was trying to find a switch, a button, something that would turn the current off. I tried to find it, and failed.

When a hand tried to restrain me, the first thing I did was to bite it. The service was interrupted. Someone shouted, 'Quick! Get a doctor!' I heard people screaming as they ran towards the door. Then something was pushed into me, probably a needle. What had been fire was rapidly transformed into fog. I am hate, fury, I thought before being engulfed. I am and am not myself. Pure destructive will.

V

They kept me in hospital for four days. The ECG revealed absolutely nothing amiss. Every morning a doctor came and asked me, 'Are you sure you didn't take anything? And perhaps drank alcohol soon afterwards?' But the analysis showed nothing.

The nuns questioned me, too. 'Did you bang your head?' And I replied, 'Certainly I did, when I fell off my bike in the Christmas holidays.' I had never been any good at lying, but all of a sudden it became easy. I found I could confuse people and manipulate them. I could put on a mask of complete innocence while the most terrible thoughts were flashing through my mind. For the first time in my life I felt safe, capable, in control. When alone I repeated over and over to myself: telling lies and holding the world in the palm of your hand are two sides of the same coin.

Back at school I became the calmest, most pious of students. I was the first to rush to the recitation of the rosary and as we said our prayers in the dormitory at bedtime my voice rose above all the others. In the chapel, mine was the only genuflection deep enough to reach the ground.

I could do this, I could afford to do this because now I knew that it was all empty sham. The crucifix was a statue and what was beneath it were only wafers. Kneeling in front of this lot was precisely the same thing as kneeling to a packet of detergent.

I now knew that my way of looking at things and my inmost thoughts were of a piece. One was steel, the other a cutting blade. Love no longer interested me; it was an idol adored by too many and, like all idols, it was hollow. The important thing was to be strong, to be able to take control of my own life and steer it in the way that would benefit me most.

Clarity of vision was my masterstroke, to see things as they are and not how one would wish them to be. Watching all those bent heads around me during Mass, I was hard put to it not to laugh out loud. When all's said and done, I thought, keeping my mouth firmly shut, true compassion must lie in understanding that they are simple souls, they know no other life than that of slaves, and that is why they have to believe that there is a God in heaven. During the Lord's Prayer I held my hands up as if expecting manna to fall into them and said, 'Our Father which art not in heaven nor in any other place . . .'

Naturally I wanted something more. I wanted complete conviction that it was all a sham. I had come a long way but the steepest path still lay ahead. That of cold-blooded sacrilege. When I had hurled Baby Jesus to the ground on Christmas Eve, I had been smoking and drinking. I was motivated by anger, not reason. Now I desired the perfect QED.

That God can kill whoever he wants and in a thousand

different ways is demonstrated throughout the Bible, in black and white. If God exists, I thought, he will punish me in some terrifying way. If he doesn't exist, nothing will happen.

One night I went to the Mother Superior's study. She had told me the truth, the door was always open. There was nothing of interest on the desk so I looked through the drawers. There I had more luck: I found a rosary worn by much use and a little wooden cross with the word 'Jerusalem' on it.

They went from my hands straight to the bowl of the loo.

Back in bed, I slept deeply and dreamlessly.

A week later the toilet was blocked. A plumber came to sort it out. He pulled out the rosary and the cross both wrapped in toilet paper like a bride in her veil.

A mantle of ice descended upon the convent. There were interrogations, sessions with the father confessor, exhaustive investigations. My ability to tell lies and the ease with which I told them surprised even myself.

For ten days no one spoke of anything else. The abused objects were re-consecrated in a special ceremony. Then that incident, too, passed into oblivion.

I was in the Mother Superior's study again at the beginning of June. It was she who summoned me. I was convinced that this was just a routine interview before the start of the summer holidays. But on the contrary, as soon as I sat down she said, 'I'm sorry, Rosa, but we cannot keep you here any longer.'

A long silence ensued. The scent of jasmine wafted in through the open window.

I should have asked 'Why?' but I had no wish to do so. When I opened my mouth I only said, 'Fine.'

'Until you are of age you will remain with your aunt and uncle . . .'

'Fine . . .'

Mother Superior came and sat opposite me. From the way she sighed I could tell she was now an old woman. Once more I felt her small, cold hands on mine.

'Is there nothing else you want to say?'

'What is there to say? It's your decision, not mine.'

'Why will you not tell me what is in your heart?'

'A heart is a box.'

'Even a box always has something inside it.'

'My box is empty.'

'Forgive me, but I don't believe that.'

'You're free to believe or not believe what you like.'

'Rosa, are you hiding something from me? I'm very worried about you.'

'As I'm about to leave, my life is no longer your business.'

'You were nearly eight years old when I held your hand in mine for the first time.'

I was beginning to feel bored.

'So what?' I said. 'Nothing lasts for ever.'

'Love lasts for ever,' she said, following me to the door. She clasped me with her thin hands.

'Remember, I'm always here and I shall be expecting you. Whatever you say to me, I'll accept it.'

She was pathetic.

'Fine,' I said drily.

'At least give me a hug and let me give you a kiss.'

I bent my head to the level of hers. Her cheeks were soft and cool.

My aunt and uncle greeted me in silence. I met their silence with my own. No one now asked me to go to church, I was no longer obliged to have good manners, they all expected the worst where I was concerned and it cost me no effort whatsoever to oblige them.

Instead of hurrying to help my aunt, I slept late every morning. I went down for breakfast when they were having their lunch. Turkey-Neck's nostrils flared with rage, but instead of attacking me she kept silent. The day I returned to the farm I had said, 'If you so much as lay a finger on me I'll create such a stink that you'll have to move away from the village.' That was why she did nothing, why she froze to the spot, kept mum and, as soon as I was out of the way, took it out on her husband. When all was said and done, I was his niece, it was he who had brought this cross into her home. The orphan child she had adopted out of Christian charity, and who should have been eternally grateful to her, had turned against her like a poison-toothed serpent.

When the heat of the day started to give way to the cooler air of evening, I took my aunt's bicycle and rode around the dusty roads. I waited for evening to watch the lizards and often stayed out to watch the stars too.

By the time I got back, my aunt and uncle had usually been asleep for some time. Even if my uncle would have preferred to stay up, my aunt still dragged him to bed with the chickens. Then I would go to the sitting room and open the drinks cupboard. There were three or four bottles that had been there for years, presents from people who were probably already dead. I began with the Vecchia Romagna brandy and continued with the Amaretto. I lay on the settee and felt warm at last. Not with the outdoor heat of the August sun but a warmth that came from inside. The same warmth that had come from the storm of kisses.

After two weeks the bottles were empty. Coming home, I needed a drink. So I began to help myself to money from my uncle's coat pockets. When he realised what was happening and hid his wallet, I began to go round the churches in the nearby villages. I carried a length of twisted wire and slipped this into the offertory boxes. After a couple of afternoons' work I always had enough to buy another bottle of alcohol.

In September I should have enrolled at a school, have forced myself in one way or another to finish my studies. In point of fact, there was only one thought in my head, my coming of age. I felt like a sprinter on the blocks, muscles tensed, eyes on the finishing-tape. I wanted to get away, far away, show everyone what I could do.

My birthday fell at the end of December. Half way through October I began to organise my escape.

The way was open when, after a month, I replied to an advertisement. A family in a nearby town was looking for an au pair. I would be required to look after their daughter, take her to school and to the swimming pool. In exchange I would have my own room and a bathroom for my exclusive use, a small wage and the chance to attend a college course. I went to meet them and we liked each other. I was to start work when they returned from a holiday in January. I naturally said nothing to my aunt and uncle, but waited for months as patiently as a spider spinning a web.

The day before my departure I bought a bottle of spumante. Before leaving the house I put it on the table with two glasses and a note. 'At last you can celebrate. Your burden is walking out on its own two legs.'

Outside it was still dark. The highroad was already busy with commuters' cars.

A bell tolled in the distance. The neighbours' dog continued to bark until it could see me no longer.

VI

Few things in this world are as delicate as house plants. A slight change of position, a microscopic draught, and a perfectly healthy-looking specimen can die in a matter of days.

The new house was full of plants. It was a penthouse on two floors with many windows in the roof. A small forest grew in every pool of light.

Giulia, the little girl's mother, loved her plants, and the first thing she did when I arrived was to show me how to look after them. As I watered them and applied shine to their leaves I couldn't help thinking about the sickly, sad, stunted plants in the convent: a dusty Golden Pothos straggling limply from the top of a cupboard, a Wandering Jew in a pot at the end of the corridor.

Plants speak of the place where they live and also of the people who live around them. In the convent they were totally neglected; here they were loved.

As the days passed I noticed that what happens to plants is not so very different from what happens to people. Living with the nuns, I was one of their plants, dull and drab, with faded leaves. With my aunt and uncle I had been a plant dying of thirst. They had bought me assuming I was made of plastic. In the new house, however, I was a plant watered with light. The light entered me and dissolved the fog, the air penetrated my pores and swept out the dust. Each morning I looked into the mirror and murmured my name. 'Rosa,' I said, as if seeing myself for the first time.

For years I had been like a pot with a lid. I boiled and boiled but there was nowhere for the steam to go. It stayed inside. Slowly it was disappearing. I heard new subjects being discussed around me, discovered a different way of dealing with life. I listened and knew that this was the right way to live, the way that should have been mine from the beginning.

For the first few days Giulia shadowed my every move. She wanted to see how I coped in the kitchen and showed me how to prepare her daughter's three or four favourite dishes. She judged my ability to help the child with her homework. Deciding after a week of this that all was well, she left me free to get on with it and returned to teaching.

We had taken to each other immediately. She treated me very affectionately and I responded to her affection by trying to do everything she asked as well as possible. I don't know exactly how old she was, but certainly over forty because she was already starting to go grey. Once, while stirring a risotto, she said, 'I only thought about having children at the last moment.' Her husband must have been about the same age. Perhaps a couple of years older. They had met at university, Giulia told me. He was now a famous architect and had a big studio where he often worked late. He was tall, with a neatly trimmed beard, always elegantly dressed, and his great love, besides architecture, was music. When he was at home the sound of his powerful stereo could be heard in every room of the house.

When I went to bed at night, before dropping off to sleep I would watch the stars, aeroplanes and satellites through the skylight. As I watched them, I fantasised about Giulia and the architect being my real parents, the ones who should have adopted me instead of my aunt and uncle. And I thought that now, even ten years later than it should have been, I had finally found my real home.

I had both lunch and supper with them and in the evening we sat together on the settee to watch television. After a few weeks I began to join in their conversations. They would ask, 'What do you think, Rosa?' and I would answer freely. No one laughed at what I said, on the contrary they showed a certain interest. For the first time I felt that my ideas were worthy of respect and didn't create a poor impression beside those of normal people.

My bedroom was an attic with sloping ceilings close to that of Annalisa, the daughter. The skylight was right above my bed, so when I couldn't sleep I could look up at the sky.

The convent and the farm now existed on a different planet; I saw them as small, faraway, inoffensive. They had disappeared from my life and were about to disappear from my memory. I had found the right family at last, the one in which I should have been born.

I would gaze at the sky and then, under the blankets, repeat the words that had always been forbidden. Papà. Mamma. Papà.

And the girl who had got drunk every evening in the living room, where had she gone? The girl who for more than ten years had lived like a prisoner either in the filth of the farm or the drabness of the convent? I could now only catch the occasional glimpse of the hate that had dominated my heart for so long. It was like a thunderstorm that, having exhausted itself in an evocation of the end of the world, suddenly falls silent and is swept away. The grass is still wet, a few trees have been set ablaze, but the storm itself is far away. That inky smudge retreating on the horizon no longer inspires fear.

The one thing that caused me a degree of annoyance in the house was the child. They had spoilt her abominably. She only had to lift a finger and point to something and it was given to her at once. Her mother was always cuddling her; she seemed to want to crush her to death. 'I know I shouldn't,' she said, 'but I can't help it. When you become parents so late in life, you are just a bit like grandparents as well.'

Annalisa was arrogant and quick-tempered. When the two of us were alone together she treated me like dirt. Naturally, I refused to let her get away with it and, if no one was looking, I squeezed her wrists hard. Not hard enough to hurt, but enough to show her who was in charge here.

One morning we went to a big department store in town to buy her some new clothes. Catching sight of myself in a mirror, I felt slightly ashamed. She was a princess, I was a Cinderella still wearing the clothes I had worn on the farm and at the convent. Under the harsh lights of the shop they revealed themselves for the rags they really were.

The assistant had to bring out dozens of dresses. While her mother tried them on her, she played up because she was bored.

'What do you think of this one, Rosa?' Giulia asked from time to time, and I gave her my opinion. Too big. Too fancy. Unsuitable.

When a dozen or so outfits had been selected and laid on the counter, the assistant asked, 'Will that be all?'

'Oh yes. That's enough,' Giulia replied.

'Now shall we see what we can do for the young lady?'

Suddenly my cheeks were burning as if I had just run a long race. The assistant had taken me for Annalisa's sister.

What would be Giulia's response? Would she say, 'Oh no, she doesn't matter, she's just a domestic?' Or . . .

I was standing with my eyes lowered when I heard her say, 'Oh yes. Now it's her turn.'

We had to go to another department. Walking through the shop I felt as if I were drunk, I was disorientated, bewildered.

The assistant slid back the door of a large cupboard. While she went through the dresses she started to chat to Giulia.

'Nowadays young people are all the same. They only want to wear cast-offs. The better the family they come from, the more they want to look like tramps. You won't believe me, Madam, but I've seen mothers imploring their daughters to accept a new dress. The fact is that we're copying everything the Americans do. The worst things of course.'

She took out a pretty pale blue cotton dress and held it against me. 'What do you think of this one? Or shall we be more daring and try something a little fancier?'

'Yes, more colourful,' Giulia said, nodding. 'Something green. Green enhances her eyes.'

I tried on four or five. Every time I came out of the fitting room I felt a different person. At one point Giulia came and swept my hair back with her fingers while looking at me in the mirror.

'See how pretty you are when you make the most of yourself!'

We came out of the shop with two packages, one for me and one for Annalisa.

For the first time in my life I started to pay attention to my appearance. Up to now I had only bothered about what went on in my head. It had never occurred to me that what others thought about me could be of any importance. I began to realise that I was neither too fat nor too thin. I was not particularly tall, but not short either. If I let my hair flow loose about my shoulders and looked in the mirror, what I saw was a pretty girl.

Shortly after our shopping trip Giulia started to insist that I should finish my interrupted schooling. Over and over again she said, 'You only have one year still to do. It would be such a pity to throw it all away. And with a brain as good as yours, you don't want to be a nursemaid all your life, do you?'

Having thought about it, I agreed with her. What sense was there in deliberately turning my back on the opportunities now presenting themselves? I was no longer restricted in what I did. I could go on to study literature or philosophy or medicine. Everyone had always expected me to come to a bad end – like my mother, they implied – but I would surprise them by becoming an important person. A great doctor. A philosopher the journalists from every paper would want to interview.

The very next week I began to attend evening classes. All the others in my class were adults and I felt very much at ease. I went there by bus, and when the lessons were over, the architect often drove me home. His studio was in the same neighbourhood and it was not unusual for him to stay there until late at night.

The first few times I was very shy. I climbed into the car without a word and remained silent throughout the journey. I didn't have the easygoing relationship with him that I did with his wife. Men had never been a part of my life – except for my uncle, who was more spectre than man. Seated next to him, however, I noticed strange things happened to me. When I replied to a question, my voice would come out either too high or too low. If he looked at me, the sweat poured from me like water from a fountain.

Did he notice my shyness? I don't know. His movements as he drove the car were all calm, measured, his attention apparently focused completely on the road. Brake, into neutral, change gear, accelerate.

Then one evening, waiting for a traffic light to change, he turned to me and said, 'Come on, tell me a bit about yourself.'

Unprepared for such a question, I stammered a few awkward sentences. In order to lie I needed time to think. Then the barrier fell and I was able to speak naturally. My father had died in an accident at work shortly before I was born. He was in the police force and had been knocked down by a runaway truck while taking measurements in the middle of a junction. My mother, on the other hand, had taught Latin. Driving home from school one day she was suddenly taken ill and the car left the road. So, at little more than seven years old, I had been left an orphan. I had an uncle and aunt, both decent, hard-working people, but they were too old to look after me. That was why I had been brought up in a convent.

Every now and then during the recitation he interposed with a comment. 'Really? . . . Good gracious! . . . What rotten luck!' When I finished, he asked, 'And did you like the convent?'

'It was lovely,' I replied. 'I had a bedroom with a bathroom all to myself, and the windows looked out over beautifully kept grounds. We had tennis courts and a covered swimming pool. It was all fine, except . . .'

'Except what?'

'I could never bring myself to believe the stories they told us.'

'What stories were those?'

'The stories told by the nuns. Jesus and all that. Heaven and hell . . . The things they invent to make people be good. To begin with I believed some of it, at least when I was very small. As soon as I grew up I realised that it was all so much eyewash.'

The architect turned round and looked at me.

'Eyewash . . .' he repeated, laughing. 'What a character!'

The following week, while I was waiting for the bus on my way to school he drove past the bus stop, pulled over, opened the door and called, 'Hop in!'

I thought he was offering me a lift, but as soon as I was in the car he exclaimed gaily, 'Today we're playing truant! We're off on a trip!'

I tried to argue, pointing out that there wasn't much time left before the exams and I didn't want to miss a lesson.

He immediately hushed me up. 'You're so bright. Nothing will happen if you miss one lesson!'

He took me to a restaurant out of town, up in the hills. As it was the end of April and still too damp to eat outside, we had a table on a kind of veranda. The tablecloth was red and white check, and very few of the tables around us were occupied. He ordered wine. I drank a glass on an empty stomach and it went straight to my head.

He sipped his slowly, looking me straight in the eyes with an unwavering stare, then, in a voice softer than usual, he said, 'You fascinate me, you know. You're so young yet so full of ideas. Tell me about yourself again, like you did the other evening.'

'What do you want to know?'

'I don't know. About the eyewash, for instance.'

I drank another glass of wine and started talking. I began at the beginning, from the Jesus with his heart in his hand who had not protected me and had protected my mother even less. I continued with the convent's crucified Christ who heard all the prayers and answered none. When they brought us the tagliatelle I had got to Don Firmato and the Christmas Mass.

The architect was so taken with what I said that he almost forgot to eat. As soon as I stopped for a second he urged me on immediately, saying, 'And then?' So I told him about the modified versions of the *Angelo di Dio* and the *Paternoster* murmured every night in the silence of my room. I then recounted every detail of the affair of the rosary and crucifix thrown down the toilet. The fact that I was still alive provided my theorem with its perfect QED. The sky was empty space.

He seemed enraptured by my story, shaking his head every now and then, at other times bursting into laughter. 'I don't believe it! Did you really do that?' Pleased with the effect, I expanded my account, adding more and more details.

Before they brought the dessert, he touched my hand very gently. 'You really are an extraordinary person, you know. You're so young yet so liberated in the way you think. I only started to see things as clearly as that just before I turned thirty. It took me until then to realise that life is only worth living if we set ourselves no restrictions. We have to open the window and throw out all restraint, all sense of guilt. Isn't that so?'

'Definitely!' I replied in a tone of finality like a teacher ending a lesson.

That night in bed, I again experienced the sensation of warmth inside. I had been without a father for so many years. Now I was happy to have had to wait so long. I could not have found a better one. The architect, whom I now called by his first name, Franco, approved of all I said, and I agreed with every word he spoke. We were truly like father and daughter.

Before falling asleep I thought that even adoption was not basically such a mad idea. My aunt and uncle would probably go to hell in the not too distant future and I should be free to become someone else's daughter. It was true they already had one daughter, but she would never be able to make them as proud of her as I could. She seemed on the dull side. And was probably too wilful, too, to make a success of anything.

Did Giulia know that the two of us went out to dinner alone every now and then? When I came home after the second time I wanted to tell her, but the words stuck in my throat, I don't know why. Even when we were together I never summoned up the courage to say, 'Yesterday evening I went out to dinner with your husband.' My relationship with both of them was strong and deep, but different in each case. For that reason I divined that it was right to keep them in separate compartments.

At the beginning of May Franco went off to lecture at a foreign university for two weeks. Throughout that time Giulia was hardly ever at home. She would phone me around seven o'clock to say, in a voice that suggested she was enjoying herself, that she would again be away for the night, and would I please give Annalisa her supper.

I felt an uneasiness that was completely new to me. I had yet to learn that love is not a silken ribbon that adorns the wrists but a steel chain that chafes them.

Having put Annalisa to bed as early as possible, I went into Franco's study to look through his things, his pens, pencils, papers. Their smell conjured up an image of his face and the warmth of his voice. Then I sat in his chair, picked up his books and opened them. They were not books on architecture but philosophy. In several there were phrases underlined. Reading them, I realised they were the same phrases that I would have underlined myself.

The evening following his return, Franco came to pick me up from school. He parked the car in a side road and pulled out two parcels.

'For you,' he said

It was the first present I had ever had since the white shirts given me by my aunt and uncle. I felt bewildered.

'Should I open them now?'

'Certainly.'

I opened the larger one first. It contained a black sweatshirt with a coloured picture of the Eiffel Tower above the word Paris on the front.

'Oh, thank you!' I said, kissing him on both cheeks. 'It's beautiful!'

Then I began to unwrap the second parcel. 'What can it be?'

He was smiling. 'Open it and see.'

The paper was burgundy red, thin as tissue, slippery to the touch. I saw two soft white objects and lifted them out. They were a brassière and a suspender-belt, both in white lace.

'Do you like them?' he asked, leaning his face close to mine. 'I saw them in a shop window and thought it possible you'd never had anything like them. Although I'm not a girl, I can imagine the pleasure of having pretty underwear. Or am I wrong?'

'I'm sure you're right.'

'You don't seem very enthusiastic.'

'Yes, I am.'

'However, if you don't like them you don't have to wear them. You can leave them sitting in a drawer or give them away.'

He re-started the engine and drove on in silence, looking straight ahead.

Perhaps, without wanting to, I had offended him. I picked up the underwear again.

'It really is beautiful! I can't wait to try it on. What is it made of, silk?'

'Yes, silk.'

The warm, scented air of May came through the open window. I wanted to gain time, make up for having offended him.

'Why don't we go for an ice-cream?' I suggested.

We were soon seated at an open-air ice-cream parlour in a residential district.

I no longer had a taste for cold, sweet things, so I ordered a whisky.

'Are you sure you're doing the right thing?' he asked. And smiled again at last.

Months had passed since I last drank spirits. Because I had eaten nothing, the whisky began to burn my stomach after the first sips. The glass seemed small, so as soon as it was empty I asked for another.

Franco took my hand in his. His fingers were tapered, his hand strong and soft and warm. Putting his lips to my ear, he murmured, 'Is there something you're trying to forget?'

There was a jasmine plant just behind us. It was in full bloom and the scent was sickly-strong. In front of us a group of lads sat astride their scooters, some smoking, others licking ice-creams.

Before speaking, I let my eyes wander to a dark point

in the night. Then I opened my mouth and began, 'My mother wasn't a Latin teacher, she was a prostitute. She was run over beside a brazier on the ring-road . . .'

That night I should have felt the relief that follows the accomplishment of a hard task. After all I had, for the first time in my life, shifted a big load from my conscience. *The* load, indeed. But instead, no sooner had I switched off the light expecting to fall into a deep, uninterrupted sleep, than I was seized by anxiety. Why had I spoken? To feel better protected? Or because I was angling for more protection? And if so, why did I feel threatened in the first place?

Even if I lacked the courage to admit it, repentance was now beginning to stir in the extreme depths of my psyche. Why had I felt the sudden urge to blurt out my secret? That secret was the well-spring of my strength, the raging willpower that allowed me to stay aloof from any attachment and overcome any obstacle. Now the secret was out in the open, known to somebody else who could make it a subject of general gossip. Perhaps Franco himself had already begun to despise me. If we met in the kitchen next day, he might not even raise his head to say 'Good morning'.

In the little square of window above my head, heavy greyish clouds appeared. Moving fast, they hid the moon and stars in only a few minutes. It'll rain tomorrow, I thought, and then I suddenly understood. Love means giving oneself utterly to the other person, with no thought of self-defence.

VII

There was less than a month to go before my exams. At table we discussed what I should do afterwards. Giulia and Franco had no objection to my continuing my studies. Annalisa was at school during the morning so I was free.

I had reluctantly abandoned the idea of architecture because mathematics was a closed book to me. The choice was between languages and philosophy.

Giulia argued for the former. If you have some languages, she said, there are so many fields open to you and you can move around, travel.

Franco, on the other hand, favoured philosophy. 'It would be a real pity to waste that brain of yours . . .' According to him, I would find my true vocation in a university philosophy department, because I enjoyed speculating on the weightiest issues and could do so with an intellectual freedom rarely found in one so young.

Franco loved this side of my character. To make him love me more, I learnt to accentuate it. I asked to borrow his philosophy books, and spent my time reading them instead of studying my school-work. Our discussions kept us up far into the night.

'You have been very privileged,' he once said, 'to grow up without love. It has enabled you to be free. You see things as they are. You don't need to construct arcane theories about them.'

'Love is a toxic substance,' he said more than once, 'because it poisons you inside, always constraining you and forcing you to do things against your will. But people like you are free. Keep it up and you'll go far. You'll carry all before you like an ice-breaker.'

'But you got married,' I retorted one day.

He burst out laughing. 'Love and marriage are anything but the same thing! People get married for money, for the company, for biological reasons, but certainly not for love. Why do you think that Giulia and I get on so well together? Because we were honest with each other from the start. We liked each other and we both wanted a child. Apart from that, we are completely free.'

I listened and nodded, nodded and listened. I never tired of talking to him. I felt superior, cut off from everything and everyone, protected by the affection of an older man, this surrogate father who was beside me.

Around the middle of June, Annalisa and Giulia went to the seaside for a week. The schools were on holiday.

The day they left, Franco took me to a friend's house for dinner. His friend was a philosophy teacher and he wanted me to talk to him about my plans for the future. I was struck by the kindness of the thought.

There was nothing I had to do in the afternoon, so I took my time getting ready. I had a long cool shower and thought carefully about what to wear. I hadn't yet worn the Parisian underwear and this seemed the ideal occasion to do so.

Before we started out, Franco suggested an aperitif on the balcony. The air was warm, full of the scents that herald the summer. House martins wheeled in their dozens above our heads, their paths criss-crossing as they darted through the air.

'As you'll see, Aldo is an amazing character,' he said. 'You'll like him. I've known him since we were boys together.'

Half an hour later we arrived at his friend's house. He too lived in a penthouse, but one without a balcony.

The first thing that struck me was his ugliness. Short, fat and bald, his face pitted with acne scars, he looked like one of those toads that hibernate under rocks. I liked him, however. He shook my hand warmly, saying, 'So this is the famous Rosa!' and then went on talking with the speed of a machine-gun. 'What wine shall we have to start with? White, red or would you prefer an Aperol or Campari? Shall we go straight to the table or relax a little first in the sitting room?'

'Rosa is the guest of honour this evening,' said Franco. 'Let her decide.'

I protested feebly. 'It's not my party,' I said.

'To some extent it is. Is it not a special day when we graduate from adolescence to adulthood?'

'In a few months' time you will be a philosophy undergraduate,' said Franco by way of clarifying the matter, 'so everything will be different.'

'Then let's have white wine,' I said, and we immediately drank a toast.

'To your studies!' they said, raising their glasses. 'To your career!'

We soon sat down to table.

Aldo was unmarried. Most of the food had been prepared the previous morning by his daily help and he had bought a few things ready-cooked.

'I apologise for being such a bad cook,' he said.

'That doesn't matter one little bit,' I said, as if I were an old friend. 'The company is the important thing.'

The wine had loosened my tongue. I can't remember what we talked about to begin with, but I do remember a particular sensation. I felt brilliant, self-confident. Where had the old Rosa gone? The hesitant, dull Rosa I had been until then? The Rosa with a chip on her shoulder?

It was as if someone had waved a magic wand and obliterated the previous eighteen years.

That evening Rosa was a charming young woman, able to hold her own in conversation with two older, more intelligent men without boring them once. Rosa was an unknown quantity even to herself. A mine full of hidden riches ready to reveal themselves if the surface were but scratched.

Towards the end of the meal Aldo asked me, 'What would you be prepared to do for a fair sum of money?'

I burst out laughing. 'Depends how much.'

'Let's say a million.'

'For a million I'd do anything.'

'Even kill?'

I was silent. I remembered my aunt hitting me with the coal-tongs. When all was said and done, killing could be a kind of pleasure. What harm would it do to the world if someone like her were to be eliminated? Even my uncle would have been happy.

'Yes, even kill.'

At that moment the telephone began to ring, but Aldo made no move to answer it.

Now it was Franco who questioned me.

'And what would you refuse to do whatever the money?'

To gain time I wiped my mouth with the table napkin, emptied my wineglass, dabbed my mouth again with the table napkin and then said, 'I would never give up my ideas. Ideas are priceless.'

Franco and Aldo insisted on clearing away without my help. 'What kind of hosts would we be if we allowed our guest of honour to clear the table?' they said. 'Go and relax for a little while in the sitting room.'

I flopped down on the sofa. My legs seemed to have

turned to jelly. I heard my friends talking merrily and laughing in the kitchen.

I, however, felt engulfed by a terrible feeling of depression. I remembered the parrot that lived in the bar in my aunt and uncle's village. It was green and sat perched on a rickety pole close to the television. Its habitual companions were drunks. The more questions they put to it, the louder it shouted. Everyone laughed at its droll answers and it flapped its wings with self-satisfaction. When the bar closed, it tucked its head under its wing and, alone and bedraggled, dozed in the lurid light of the neon sign.

What had triggered this feeling of sadness, of depression? Was it the farm? The convent? The fact that my mother was no more? Was it true that she was no more, or was she still there, somewhere? My eyes were becoming perilously moist. I threw my head back as one does to put in eye-drops and was surprised to see my reflection on the ceiling.

The whole ceiling was one large mirror.

'What is that for?' I asked as soon as they came back.

'To show up the dust!' replied Franco.

Aldo laughed. 'Don't believe him. The mirror is there so that I can make sure no one tries to walk off with anything. I've got a lot of valuable books in this room and small objects too. Nice things are always a temptation.'

While speaking he had fetched a packet of cigarette papers and begun to mix a dark substance with tobacco on a large illustrated volume. Franco sat down beside me and put his arm round my neck. He was wearing lightweight trousers, and his thigh lay tight against mine.

'A good party, eh?'

'Wonderful,' I replied, but all I could think about now was the parrot. At least, when the time came, he could be alone. Where had she gone, the Rosa of earlier this evening? I could no longer reach her. The only Rosa now was the one who wanted to cry.

When they passed me the cigarette I inhaled deeply. Aldo sat close to me on the other side. My head began to spin violently. It was no longer tears that threatened to spill out, but vomit. The food I had eaten heaved in my stomach and throat as if I were being tossed in a small boat on a rough sea.

Whose was that hand, damp and pulpy? Whose was that voice? It seemed to come from far away. What was it saying? Why did it mention my mother? I opened my hand and found it contained a banknote. I gripped it tightly as if it were a handle to hold on to. Was I sitting or lying down? I was in no state to determine. Something heavy was pressing down on me, I wanted to push it away but my arms had no strength in them. So I did what hunters do when confronted by a dangerous bear. I pretended to be dead.

Some time before, Annalisa and I had watched a documentary about training dogs. At first the dogs romped about, happy and disobedient. By the end of the course all playfulness had been knocked out of them; they did nothing but respond to commands: 'Get up! Sit! Lie! Pick it up! Put it down! Stay! Turn round!' The instructor spoke in a loud voice. If this failed to produce the desired effect, he used a whistle. If the whistle also failed, he used electric shocks. Administered through an electrode in the collar, they made the animal tremble and whine with pain.

VIII

That night and the following nights I had the same dream. I am in a big, empty house, a house full of rooms and passages. Although there are tools lying around, some bricks, a bricklayer's trowel, a brush and a pot of paint, it seems to have been abandoned long since. The floor-boards creak, cobwebs hang from the walls and door-posts. Why am I here? I ask myself, but do not know the answer. So I venture further. I walk slowly, cautiously, constantly testing the floor before treading on it. I don't know where to go, but I am clearly looking for a way out. And just as I come down some stairs I hear the voice of a child. Not playing or laughing, but crying. 'What's happening?' I call out in the emptiness of the house. 'Someone find it! Someone help it!' In that instant I notice that somewhere in the house a fire has broken out. The walls are of wood and smoke is already billowing through the passages. The child's voice is increasingly desperate. Instead of saving myself, I run to find it. I rush up to the next floor, and the one above, reach the attics, then run down to the cellar. There are no longer dozens of doors but hundreds and they are all shut. The crying shifts from one to another. The flames follow me like a pack of dogs. Then the cries become clearer, more comprehensible, I know now that someone in the house is harming the child. There are three doors in front of me and a voice says, 'You may open only one of them. Choose but be quick.' I choose the one to the left, stretch out my hand to open it and then realise that instead of arms I have tentacles. Not strong tentacles like an octopus but soft, slippery ones like a jellyfish. Even so, I push them towards the handle, they feel like overcooked spaghetti, they curl around it for a moment or two, then slide off. The heat in the passage is almost unbearable. Jellyfish cannot survive heat. I feel my tentacle-legs already buckling beneath me. I'm going to die by melting, I think, and at that moment I notice that there is a man on top of me. Was it he who took me out of the water? Or has he come to help me? By now I am lying completely collapsed on the floor. The child is crying harder than ever. I want to put my hands over my ears, but I have no ears. Looking at the man I see that he has dark eyes and is carrying a harpoon. He raises it and thrusts at me. I feel the point pass through my body and pin me to the floor. A second before I die I realise that the child's voice is my own.

The next day I woke up in the empty house. Franco came home in the early afternoon.

'Why the long face?' he asked as soon as he saw me.

'I've got a headache.'

'That comes from mixing your wines.'

He gave me a tablet and soon afterwards went out again. I stayed in the house all afternoon and all evening as well. The telephone rang once, it was Giulia.

'Is something wrong?' she asked on hearing my voice.

'A nasty headache.'

'That'll be the stress of your exams.'

After hanging up I took a bottle of vodka from the fridge and drank it as if it were water, then lay on the settee in front of the television until I felt strong enough to drag myself to bed. I had already been lying there half-asleep for some time when I heard Franco's breathing. He smelt of wine and garlic. He was on top of me.

'No,' I said softly.

'Why not?'

'I'm tired.'

'As long as I'm not tired it doesn't matter.'

Who said that you only see shooting stars in August? Lying there with my eyes open, I saw a particularly bright one flash across the sky. What shall I wish for? I wondered. But it was already too late, the star had vanished.

Two days later it was Aldo who came to supper with us. I could have escaped, but I didn't. Where could I have gone to hide?

I began to drink early in the afternoon. By suppertime I could barely stand. I only remember that we laughed a lot. At one point I heard myself say, 'To do this, I want at least three times as much money!'

I laughed so much my cheeks were wet with tears.

When Giulia returned, my face, from my neck to my cheeks, was covered with pimples. I draped a cloth over the bathroom mirror so that I couldn't see myself.

'You get too emotional,' she scolded me affectionately. 'It's not worth working yourself up into such a state for the sake of an exam which is not that important after all.'

To allow me to study in peace she kept Annalisa with her all day. I sat in my room with my books open in front of me and drank vodka. Then I scrubbed my teeth and chewed mints so that they would notice nothing.

To avoid being alone with Franco I went everywhere with Giulia. If there were too long a silence I immediately filled it with chatter. I was afraid she would come out with the truth, that she would suddenly ask, 'What's happened between you and my husband?'

However, for the moment she apparently suspected nothing, and she continued to treat me as affectionately as ever. Perhaps it would have been wiser to confide in her and tell her exactly how things stood. But I was afraid of losing her too, and that I couldn't have borne.

One evening Franco blocked my way as I went upstairs. I

61

had been down to fetch a bottle of wine from the kitchen. They had guests to dinner and everyone was outside, eating on the balcony. He pressed me hard against the wall, I felt the hardness of his body against the fragility of mine. His lips were level with my eyes, and I saw them move as he whispered, 'Don't you want to enjoy yourself any more?'

'I'm about to scream.'

On the first of July, like all the other students, I left the house clutching my dictionary ready for the written exam. As I went down the steps, Giulia opened the door and called out, 'Good luck!' – 'Thanks!' I replied as I got to the bottom.

Sitting in front of the blank sheet of paper, I filled it from top to bottom with a single phrase written over and over again. 'I don't know what to write, I don't know what to write, I don't know what to write . . .' When every last line had been filled I got up, gave in my paper and left the room. As it was still early I walked around the town for a bit before going home.

When it was time for the second exam, mathematics, I didn't even bother to go to the school. I left the house at the right time and took a succession of buses in order to avoid being seen. I had a meal in a bar, then walked around the nearby streets. In an unfrequented street a car drew up beside me. In it was a big man with a broken nose.

'Where are you off to all alone?' he said, leaning out of the open window.

'I don't know where I'm going,' I replied furiously, 'but you can go to hell.'

The man swore and drove off with a squeal of tyres.

I felt swollen. I was on edge. My period was a week

late. It's the stress of the exams, I told myself, but without conviction.

In the second week of July, Giulia and Annalisa went off again to the seaside, and this time Franco went with them. My oral exams were now due.

On the morning of the exam I stayed at home and did a pregnancy test.

The result was positive.

Aldo phoned during the afternoon. 'I know you're there on your own,' he said. 'Would you like me to come and keep you company?'

I slammed down the phone without answering.

So now what? Something was growing inside me in the same way that I had grown inside my mother.

I thought with nostalgia of the dim light of the convent, of that world in which everything had its rightful place. You can never go back. They say there's always light at the end of a tunnel, but if the tunnel is blind there is only a more impenetrable darkness at the end.

I was groping my way in that darkness, and I knew that the darkness was no figment of the imagination. However much I punched, kicked, shouted incantations, I would never be able to force open the smallest chink to the light outside. Perhaps from the very beginning I had chosen the fate of the mouse that loses its way and rather than climb upwards goes deeper and deeper until it collides with a wall of rock.

Was there anyone who could help me?

My aunt and uncle were out of the question. I could just see Turkey-Neck crowing triumphantly, 'I said you were the same as your mother, capable only of . . .'

My one remaining hope lay with Mother Superior.

But how could I find the words to tell her that I was expecting a baby and did not know who the father was?

I spent the next three days drinking and weeping on every sofa in the house. At last I made up my mind and dialled the convent's number. Hadn't she said that she would accept whatever I told her?

'Mother Superior is not here,' the telephonist replied.

'When can I speak to her?' I asked, disguising my voice to avoid recognition.

'She's been in hospital for the last two months. She's very ill.'

End of conversation.

While waiting for Franco's return I began to have very hot baths and pummel my stomach violently. There was a kind of spider in there, and it was growing. Day after day its hairy legs were getting longer. First it would invade my bladder, then the intestines. From there it would get into the stomach and then take over the liver. I would feel it even getting to my throat. Perhaps it was no longer a spider but a bat, a creature of the night. Like everything that lives in the dark, it had no need of eyes, it would be born blind, with empty eye-sockets. That was why I did everything I could to prevent it from being born.

They got back on Sunday evening.

While Giulia was unpacking I went to Franco and told him, 'I'm pregnant.'

He stood motionless for a second, looking me in the eyes.

'Are you sure?'

'Yes.'

'Don't worry, it's a minor accident. The one responsible for it will put it right.'

64

The next day Giulia asked me, 'So? Did you pass?'

'Yes,' I replied, 'with forty-eight per cent.'

She insisted on celebrating that evening. She bought an ice-cream cake and a bottle of spumante. After we had all drunk the toast together I burst into tears.

'Why is she crying?' asked Annalisa, putting on her baby voice. Franco was gazing out of the window. Giulia put her arms round me.

'Rosa's crying because she's too sensitive for her own good.'

The following week, Franco made an appointment with a friend of his in a clinic.

'You'll see, it's less serious than having a tooth out.'

Sleep was now impossible. In summer the attic was like an oven. Even with the roof-window wide open it was impossible to breathe. I would have a shower and then another immediately afterwards. My stomach and breasts had begun to swell. 'It suits you with a little more flesh on your bones,' observed Giulia.

In the silence of the night I gazed at the stars. If you thought about it, the sky was so big there just might be Someone up there. Alone, with that thing growing inside me, I wanted to pray. I used to think that only the weak and stupid needed Him. Now I realised that I had been right. I had been stupid and now I was weak, that was why I cried aloud to Someone, asking Him to appear on the threshold of the universe. As there's no one else to help me, You help me!

I was ashamed of these thoughts, of my hypocrisy. I was treating Him like an insurance company. After all that I had said and done, how could I ever turn to Him? Any invocation of mine would bounce off the door of heaven like a tennis ball off a wall.

Perhaps Don Firmato had been right after all and I was

truly the spawn of Satan. Perhaps the best solution would really have been for my aunt to kill me with her bare hands that evening. She had not been mistaken when she detected the smell of sulphur. With whom had my mother conceived me? And with whom had I conceived my child?

I looked at the sky and couldn't squeeze out a tear. I looked at the sky and couldn't utter a prayer.

I don't know why, but my lips shaped a word. A word I had never spoken. Forgive.

One night I had a dream. It was no longer a spider in my womb but a tiny point of light. Instead of staying still, it whirled around throwing its rays into the darkness. I had never seen such a clear, intense, pure light.

Next morning I awoke with a strange noise in my ears. As I showered, I thought it must be caused by low pressure. The noise was still there in the afternoon. It wasn't the usual whistling noise, but seemed more like the sound of the sea, the sound you can hear in a shell or listening to waves breaking on a shore.

There were only two days to go before my appointment at the clinic. What was I to do with this child I didn't want? How could I ever care for someone with Aldo's, or Franco's, face? I would hate it, I would try to destroy it the very first day. Instead of milk, I would give it poison to drink.

Perhaps my mother had felt the same about me, had thought of throwing me down the toilet but had not done it. I was now the one regretting her decision. My life was one long blunder. It would have been better, much better, had I never been born.

The morning I was due at the clinic, Franco gave me the taxi fare. I was to use it for the return journey. The clinic was right on the outskirts of town. I started very early to be in good time. When I got off the bus there was still an hour to go until my appointment.

Rather than go in early, I walked around the neighbouring streets for a while. There were some newly built houses, uncultivated fields, four or five barns and, almost squeezed in between them, a small church. It must have been there long before the town was built. The day was already scorching. The door was ajar. Thinking of the coolness inside, I pushed it open and went in. The place was small and very plain, with a tiled floor like a dentist's surgery.

An ugly figure of Christ on the Cross had pride of place behind the altar. The Christ was not yet dead but suffering the full horror of the Agony. He was twisted, writhing as though the pain were gnawing his bones. The flowers in the two vases underneath were, by contrast, already dead. They stood limply, flabbily, in the dirty water.

On the right-hand side of the altar was a statue of the Virgin Mary wearing a crown of little lights of the kind you see on gondolas and the usual long blue mantle. Her arms were open wide as if she were waiting to welcome somebody. She wore no shoes, but that hadn't stopped her from crushing the head of a serpent with her naked foot.

Two lighted candles flickered in front of her.

They're about to go out, I thought, and just then some sparrows flew in through a broken windowpane, twittering loudly as they chased each other playfully through the air. They flew about making a lot of noise for a few moments, then perched on the arms of the cross.

They were not playfellows, however, but a mother sparrow with her fledgling brood. The youngsters now began chirping and flapping their wings and their mother fed them, thrusting her beak into their tiny gaping throats. They asked and she gave, feeding them even though they were already big enough to fly.

The Virgin with her gentle smile was still watching me. Her cheekbones were a shade redder than the rest of her face.

I raised my eyes to her and said, 'Should You not be the mother of us all?'

Then I stretched out my hand to touch the foot that was crushing the serpent. I had expected it to be cold, but it was warm.

Half an hour later I was on the couch in the clinic. The doctor who was Franco's friend was smearing gel on my abdomen in preparation for an ultrasound scan. The sound of the sea was still there. *Tumf, sfloosh, tumf, sfloosh, tumf, sfloosh.*

'Doctor,' I said, 'is it possible that I could be hearing my child's heartbeat already?'

He burst out laughing. 'What a vivid imagination!' He pointed to a dot on the screen. 'What you call your child is not, at the moment, very different from a blob of spit.' Then he said, 'Put your clothes back on and make yourself comfortable in the next room. In half an hour we can proceed.'

I dressed and settled down to wait. All of a sudden, as I sat there, I smelt my mother's scent. The scent of her skin and her eau-de-Cologne. The scent I had not smelt for years. The scent of the storm of kisses. I looked around. There was no one else in the room, and the windows were shut. So I understood and did the only thing I could do. I got up and walked away.

There was a public phone near the bus stop. I dialled Franco's number. He was in his studio.

'How are you?' he asked.

'I'm fine because I've decided to keep it.'

'Have you gone mad?'

'Perhaps.'

'Do you want to be responsible for bringing another hapless individual into the world?'

'Perhaps.'

There was a long silence, then he said, 'I would never have expected such idiotic behaviour from you. Still, you're free to ruin your life. It remains to be seen whether or not I choose to ruin mine as well.'

My pregnancy was still not visible, but it would be before long. What would I do then?

I was turning this over in my mind a few days later when, going into the kitchen, I found them both confronting me with stony, livid faces.

'What's happened?' I asked almost inaudibly, ready for the worst.

Giulia's voice was shaking.

'How could you do this to me?'

I lowered my eyes. Was this how he had decided to avenge himself?

'It's true. I should have said something before now.'

'Should have said what? That you were a thief? I treated you like a daughter! I've been looking for my emerald ring for days on end and where do I find it? At the bottom of one of your drawers! I wonder how many other things have "gone missing" over these past few months!'

'We made the mistake of trusting her,' added Franco, his expression inscrutable. 'But when the root is rotten the tree will rot sooner or later. We were fond of you, however, and for that reason we shall not call in the police. But I must ask you to leave this house before noon tomorrow. And, of course, to give back everything that does not belong to you.'

The umpteenth night without sleep. Instead of resting I spent the hours wondering how best to take my revenge. The absence of light is conducive to the most horrendous thoughts.

I wanted to suffocate his daughter with a pillow, push her into the canal, watch her golden hair floating on the water like dirty rags. I wanted to empty a can of petrol over the parquet floor and wooden furniture and then throw matches into it and burn him alive like an Indian woman on her husband's pyre. I wanted to tamper with the brakes on his car and see him crash into a wall. I wanted to spit in his face and then thrust a knife into his stomach. I wanted to slit him open from his chin to his belly like a tunnyfish and draw out his still-warm intestines with my own hands. I wanted to make him drink poison, a slow-acting poison that would cause an unbearably agonising death.

Then the thought occurred to me that death was a blessing, that it would be far better if he lived in humiliation and torment. He could break his back falling down the stairs and spend the rest of his days in bed, gagged by a respirator. Or a house he had designed could collapse with great loss of life so that he would be sent to prison and lose everything. By the time he came out his wife would have gone off with another man and his daughter, now a grown woman, would pretend not to know him. So he would end up on the streets, going from one soup-kitchen to the next with his plastic carrier-bags.

I could have told his wife, too, that I had stolen nothing from her. Admittedly I was full of hatred, but my hatred had nothing to do with greed. I could have told her the plain and simple truth behind the story of the theft. I could have told her what her husband got up to those nights when he worked late at the office. I could have told her that the child growing inside me was probably Annalisa's brother or sister and that we were about to become, in a way, related.

I could have told her all this, but she might not have believed me. Indeed, she certainly would not have believed me, a homeless girl, daughter of a prostitute who stole and drank, when the man I was accusing was her husband. The man who provided her with a comfortable lifestyle, the father of the child who was the light of her life. Silence was easier to bear than disbelief.

Shortly before dawn I got my sports bag out of the cupboard and packed it with the few belongings I had had when I arrived.

Before leaving the house I slipped a note into Giulia's handbag. It read, 'One day you will understand. Forgive me. Rosa'.

It was the beginning of August and the town was deserted. A water-lorry from the department of public hygiene moved slowly along the street hosing the pavements. Great flocks of house martins chirruped loudly among the rooftops. A cat with a red collar crossed the road. Having nowhere to go, I found myself in a nearby park. It was the coolest place I knew. A few elderly people were walking their dogs there and a few young ones were taking advantage of the freshness for a morning jog.

I sat down on a secluded bench. Close by, a pair of doves was sitting on a wrought-iron drinking fountain, taking it in turns to stretch their necks towards the trickle of water. I could see their crops fill and the liquid slide down their throats.

Further away, an old lady with her feet wrapped in plastic bags was rummaging through the contents of a rubbish bin, sniffing things and then throwing them back. Her expression was calm, almost amused. Perhaps there had been a time when she was a woman of consequence, had borne children and men had been in love with her.

I had always wondered what love is, but never what life is. We come into this world and our existence is nothing if not precarious. It takes no more than a moderately malevolent virus or a blow on the head to dispatch us to the hereafter.

Precarious and an open invitation to evil, an evil that we perpetrate upon each other. This invitation we have accepted since the world began. We accept it out of obedience, passion, laziness or heedlessness. I kill you to live. I kill you to possess. I kill you to be free of you. I kill you because I love power. I kill you because you are worthless. I kill you because I want revenge. I kill you because I enjoy killing. I kill you because you annoy me. I kill you because you remind me that I too may be killed.

Everything in this world has its opposite. North and south. High and low. Hot and cold. Male and female. Light and darkness. Good and evil. But then, if that is really so, how come I can say 'I'll kill you' but not 'I'll give you back your life?' Life was before man was, and no man is capable, by an act of will, of creating life. We can cry 'Die!' but not 'Live!' Why? What does this mystery hide?

While I was thinking about these things, a dog came up to me. He looked quite old, his coat patchy and greyish-white, his belly swollen with malnutrition, his eyes covered with a milky film. He sat down painfully beside me. His mouth hung open and he was panting heavily.

'I haven't got any food to give you,' I told him, but he stayed.

The sun began to beat down upon my head, so I went to sit under a big horse chestnut. Its spreading branches provided a cool shade, hundreds of insects buzzed around beneath the leaves.

The dog followed me. There was no bench here, so I sat on the ground. He lay down beside me. His breathing sounded like a bellows.

'Do you want me to stroke you?' I asked, resting my hand on his head. He closed his eyes with what looked like an expression of happiness.

The sky above us was as blue as an enamelled goblet. The house martins had gone, now only the occasional dove flew ponderously past. High up, the silver belly of an aeroplane shone like a herring. Then it vanished, leaving a streak of white behind it, as long and straight as a country road.

Are there paths in the sky? I wondered. Where do they lead? Who makes them?

The dog put his paw in my hand.

'Does Someone lead us, or are we on our own?' I asked him.

His eyes were half-shut, his tongue lolling. He seemed to be smiling.

'Answer me.'

No Such Thing as Hell

I

I HAVE RETURNED TO my parents' house, that house you detested for so long. I had a struggle to open the door, the lock was rusty and the wood swollen after so much rain.

When I eventually succeeded it was like walking into a museum. Or a burial vault. Everything was in its place. The air was cold and damp with that chill humidity that preserves things no longer alive from the ravages of time. The tablecloth was still on the kitchen table. On it, a jug and a glass. There were ashes in the fireplace. My mother's thick-lensed glasses rested on the arm of her chair beside a ball of wool with two knitting needles stuck through it. Our wedding photo sat enthroned on top of the television. There we are, leaving the church arm in arm, you in a morning suit, me in a long white dress. Someone must have laughed just at that moment, because you are smiling and so am I. But I am smiling with my eyes shut.

It was my mother who chose that photo. There were much better ones. I showed them to her several times, but she dug her heels in. 'I want this one,' she said, jabbing it with an arthritic finger. I tried to dissuade her. 'Isn't this a nicer one? Or this?' – 'No, no, this is the one

I want.' – 'But why this one specifically?' – 'Because here you are really yourself.' I dusted the photograph by rubbing it with my sleeve. Spiders had begun to spin their webs in the corners of the frame.

At the time I had asked myself what made that photo so different from all the others. I had asked, but found no answer. Now, in the unnatural silence of the house, the answer came to me. It was because my eyes were closed. I was walking down those steps blindly, relying on your arm to guide me. I had no doubts about the sureness of your guidance.

'You only see what you want to see,' my father said shortly before his death. It was twilight and he was standing in front of the stable. He died two months later. One evening the dog returned alone. At dawn the next day they found him lying in a patch of moss. Some animal had already begun to nibble his ears.

It was the beginning of September. We were sailing towards the Costa Smeralda. 'Your father's dead,' you said, coming on deck. 'The funeral is tomorrow or the day after. You won't get there in time.'

My mother died while we were in Singapore, where you had business. No one in the village knew where I was, so no one could let me know. I heard about it when we got home.

When I went to the cemetery, grass was already growing on the freshly disturbed earth. It was May, and the ditches were still full of snow. The streams, swollen with water, leapt between the rocks. The larches were covered with soft, pale-green needles. The same luminous green of the meadows. At the time, I was unable to feel any deep emotion. Perhaps I was still anaesthetised by your presence. Rather than living, I was watching myself live.

Then, luckily, you died too.

When I found you that morning, lying on the bathroom floor, it was much the same as seeing an insect there.

When we were still engaged you made me read Kafka's *Metamorphosis*. You enthused about it. 'In here', you said repeatedly, 'is the whole essence of modern man.' To please you, I pretended to enthuse about it too. 'It makes me shiver,' I said. It was only half a lie, because the shivers were real enough. But they were shivers of disgust.

Seeing you lying there naked, spread-eagled, the flabbiness of age stiffening in rigor mortis, it was he, Gregor Samsa, who came into my mind. I didn't touch you, but I am sure that had I done so I would have felt not flesh but the chitinous exoskeleton of a beetle beneath my foot.

The following week was the most difficult. I had to don the mask of the distraught widow. You had been an important man and everyone wanted to express condolences. When I could bear the ritual phrases no longer, I retreated to the bathroom and do you know what I did? I burst out laughing. I laughed till the tears ran down my cheeks, I laughed with the carefree joyousness of an adolescent. I laughed like a new lottery-winner who has to keep his win a secret.

Your obituary took up two columns in the local paper. 'He leaves a wife and daughter,' they wrote at the end. Not one single word about the other child. When someone dies, everything he leaves behind becomes good. Isn't this the ultimate insult for those who must go on, dragging with them the burden of memory?

Once the farce was over I had but one thought in my mind, about how happy my widowhood was going to be. You had left me a tidy sum in the bank, and my native curiosity and the interests of my youth were still intact. I wanted to travel and learn foreign languages, enrol in a course of watercolour painting, join a literary society. I would never again allow anyone to dictate to me. I had to make up for lost time so that when I died I would have the serene expression of a person with no regrets.

How could I have been so ingenuous? Evil is many-faceted and insinuates itself everywhere with mimetic cunning. It may seem to die, but it always rises again. Your heart had failed, but your spirit lived on. A vindictive, destructive spirit, a spirit of hate for everything capable of escaping your rule of humiliation.

At the age of fifty-five we can no longer delude ourselves that life is still before us, that we can enjoy it as if we were babies. Some of it is in the past, and the past dictates the future.

Picking up my mother's knitting, her thick-lensed, old-lady glasses covered in dust, I understood one thing. Retreating armies usually destroy bridges. You did the same where my life was concerned. With obsessive attention to detail you destroyed everything that was behind me. Then, to prevent me from ever lifting my head again, you laid mines all along the way ahead.

This deserted house and I are now one and the same. The walls are crumbling with damp. When it rains, water leaks in all over the place. Woodpeckers have reduced the shutters to colanders while the mice have gnawed everything gnawable, electric wires, stubs of candles, the Bible on the bedside table and the old magazines kept for lighting the fire, the dusters and the pillowcases folded neatly in the settle in the hallway.

The first evening I felt very depressed. Wearing an overcoat and carrying a candle I wandered from one room to another. Everything was in such a state of disrepair that any idea of putting it right within days and with no one to help seemed out of the question. To survive the first few nights I had brought one of the children's sleeping bags with me. I went to my parents' bedroom, but couldn't bring myself to lie on their bed. They had found my mother there, lying face-down on the floor with one arm stretched out in front of her and one behind, like a swimmer.

'Was death instantaneous?' I asked the local GP.

'Who knows?' he answered with a shrug of his shoulders. 'I could put your mind at rest by saying yes, she lost consciousness after three minutes, but what would it mean? The concept of time for a dying person is very different from ours. What would be a moment for us is an eternity to them.'

Now that I am alone in the house, it is precisely that idea of eternity that frightens me. If she didn't die immediately, what thoughts would have passed through her mind in those last seconds? Perhaps she was trying to reach the phone, which would explain why she was lying there with her arm outstretched. Perhaps she was thinking of calling me but never made it. Or perhaps she knew that it would be completely useless.

When was the last time I went to see her? It was shortly after my father's death, so it must have been two years ago. How far was their home from ours? A car journey of about three and a half hours, four if the traffic was heavy.

When the children were little I used to take them there for at least a month every summer and two weeks in the winter. The old sledge my grandfather had made was still there, and we all clambered aboard to go and do the shopping. When we braked, the snow flew into our faces, making us all look like snowmen.

Then, as the children grew up, Laura started to want to be like all the others and holidays in the snow with granny and grandpa were no longer good enough for her. She wanted ski schools and chairlifts, discos in the evening. Not so Michele. Michele was always different. He loved the house in the mountains. As a tiny boy with a round blond head he would follow his grandfather everywhere. When he was five my father made him a little flute by whittling a reed. The sound of piping would rise unexpectedly from the most improbable places. It got on everyone's nerves but to Michele it must have sounded wonderful and he repeated the same notes over and over again. Sometimes I would see him sitting on a bale of straw or in the cubby-hole under the stairs, frowning as if he were thinking some very serious thoughts.

You never liked his eyes.

'They're not blue,' you said, 'nor green. Even the colour is muzzy.'

His eyebrows and eyelashes irritated you; they were too dark, too pronounced. 'They look painted on,' you said, pointing at him as if he were an animal for sale in the market place.

When he was seven or eight you often used to tell him, 'You look like Bambi's floozy.'

Later, when he acquired the gangly limbs of adolescence and lost his childish prettiness, your favourite refrain was, 'With that makeup you could pass for a tart any day.'

Shortly before coming here I heard a priest on television say that hell did not exist. I was busy at the time and not paying much attention, but a couple of days later I read the same statement in a serious daily paper.

There is no such thing as hell, according to this writer,

whose statement was corroborated by a well-known theologian. Or if it exists at all, it is certainly empty. I was alone in the house, and began to pace through the rooms banging the newspaper against the furniture. 'You bastards! You liars!' I screamed. 'So where is Hitler, then? And Stalin? Playing harps in the empyrean? Or are they brushing the cherubs' curls? If hell is empty, I at least want to go there. Be left in peace in the warmth of the flames, all alone as in a big hotel out of season!'

Once I had calmed down I thought now they really are scraping the bottom of the barrel. No one listens to them any more, they've lost their congregations. Courting popularity they've torn down the last barriers. Do as you like, commit any abomination, after all, no one will be excluded from the banquet. Joy, love and eternal life for all. The medical missionary and the child-abuser seated side by side. What a party!

If hell doesn't exist, nothing exists. Not only must it exist, it must be utterly cut off from the upper regions. There must be barbed-wire fences and flames and jagged bits of broken glass and high-tension wires and hermetically sealed compartments, a vacuum without air or atmospheric pressure and a gaping black hole to swallow anyone who tries to get out. It is inconceivable that my mother and father could ever be anywhere near you, or could even imagine that you still exist in any corner of the universe. That is why it is necessary to have all those barriers between what is below and what is above.

I slept the first night in the bed I had slept in as a girl, in the converted attic. It was hardly sleeping, more a case of waiting for dawn in a horizontal position. I never lost consciousness for an instant. The house was full of life. Some of the noises I recognised, mice running across the floor, the scrabbling of weasels and polecats as they lifted roof-tiles looking for their nests, wooden furniture creaking as it swelled and shrank adjusting itself to the temperature. At some point during the night the wind got up. It must have been a north wind since it was buffeting the north side of the house. Outside, something metallic tinkled, sounding like shrouds rattling against the mast of a sailing ship. I heard the kitchen window blow open with a bang. Without going downstairs I could still imagine the gust of wind blowing in and scattering things about, the ball of wool rolling off the chair, the sheets of newspaper kept for lighting the fire fluttering across the room, the curtain under the kitchen sink billowing out and the souvenir gondola beside the clock on the mantelpiece rocking. Everything, suddenly, had a life of its own. Grandmother's photograph on the dresser, her voice saying, 'Those who die alone stay down here seeking company. They pace backwards and forwards like animals in a cage.'

When the gust had died down, I thought I heard footsteps. Whose footsteps were they? It sounded like an old person shuffling about in slippers.

II

The hotel where we met no longer exists. The old proprietors are dead and their only heir, a nephew in Australia, never cared to take it over. The name is still there, or at least part of it. On a corner of the main road you can still see 'Al . . . chio . . . rpone'. 'Al vecchio scarpone', 'At the Sign of the Old Boot'.

You were staying there to keep your sister company. She was recovering from a chest infection. You both stayed all summer and you were bored to death. Every now and then the eleven o'clock coach would bring some parcels for you. They contained books. When it rained you passed the time reading in your room. When the weather was good you did exactly the same, sitting on a bench or lying on the grass.

I could hardly avoid noticing you. I was in my last year at school before going on to teacher-training college, earning a little during the summer by helping out at the hotel. You struck me as being different from all the other young men I knew. At the August bank holiday festival I had danced with a corporal in the Alpine Regiment and felt nothing. The only male in our class was the laughing-stock of all the girls. But when my eyes met yours I blushed for no reason at all.

I was convinced that you would never notice me. Then one evening, as I was walking past the creaky swing-seat, you asked me to sit down. You talked to me for a long time about a variety of subjects, like people do when they are feeling very lonely. I couldn't understand everything you said. Yours was more a philosophical dissertation than a conversation, and my limited education as an aspiring school-teacher had not equipped me to follow such arguments.

At our first meeting I was grateful for your attention. By the third my gratitude had become pride. You used the formal 'lei' mode of address as if I were a person of consequence.

After a week, lifting my hair from my shoulders, you murmured, 'Blue eyes and black hair, red lips and skin as white as new-fallen snow. Has anyone ever told you that you are very beautiful?'

No, no one had ever said that.

Nor had anyone ever spoken to me like you did when I came to see you off on the coach.

'Are you going to spend the rest of your life up here in

the mountains teaching a handful of children suffering from goitre?'

Instead of replying, I stammered a few confused words.

'Hasn't it ever occurred to you that you could get much more out of life?'

'More what?'

You were standing on the top step, the automatic doors were about to shut.

'Everything! If you wanted, you could have everything!'

The following summer you returned for a couple of weeks, this time without your sister. We went for long walks hand in hand. We always sought out the solitary, romantic spots, far from prying eyes. We would sit under the big willow by the stream or in a clearing among the larches. And there, instead of trying to kiss me as others did, you would take a book out of your pocket and read poetry to me.

In your company I began to see myself in a different light. I began to understand more, to think more deeply. I was grateful to you for sharing the bold flights of your intellect with me.

Eventually, that boldness made me restless. I was no longer content with the life I had lived up to then. The life that lay before me in the valley now seemed no better than a kind of imprisonment.

We became engaged in September of that year, and were married in September of the year after.

My father disliked you. My mother, however, made an effort to defend you. 'What harm has he done to you, poor lad? You've taken against him simply because he's a city boy!' My father's head sank between humped shoulders. 'That's not it,' he said, whittling away nervously at a piece of wood. 'So what is it then?' she asked stubbornly. 'I don't know,' he muttered, 'but I don't like him.' And his head sank even lower.

By our wedding day I had already learned to be ashamed of them. The reception was held in the garden of your parents' house. Huge marquees shaded tables heaped with food. Waiters were everywhere, carrying trays in white-gloved hands. Wandering about bemused among the guests, my father and mother looked like extras who had turned up for the wrong film.

When the time came to cut the cake, my father raised a hand as if to ask for silence. But instead of making a speech, he pulled out his old mouth-organ from a jacket pocket and began to play an extremely mournful song. At that moment I felt my distaste for him become a real physical force. 'Papa, that's enough!' I whispered to him after a couple of minutes of torture. But he, unheeding, carried on for what seemed an eternity.

Among the guests some sighed, others smothered a laugh. The laughter exploded into guffaws when your father's hunting dogs arrived on the scene and began to accompany him with their howls.

Honeymoon in Vienna, dinner with a gypsy fiddler playing just for us, and then the bedroom. During our engagement we had only kissed, lightly brushing each other's lips. I was touched by your refined sensitivity.

You shut the door and gripped my wrists. Your eyes, unblinking, were like deep wells that have been covered up for years.

'Do you know what marriage is?' you asked, tightening your grip.

'Two people loving each other' is what I wanted to say, but instead I murmured, 'Let go, you're hurting me.'

'Marriage is a contract. Now, and for ever, you will be my chattel.'

Who was this man I had married?

III

I opened the windows to air the rooms. There were plenty of logs in the shed behind the stable. Finding the log-basket still in good repair, I filled it and made two or three trips.

Only old people live in the village now. Some greeted me, others pretended not to see me.

The church has been abandoned for many years. A priest comes from the valley only once a year, for the Feast of the Assumption in August, and is off and away in his little car before the damp gets to his bones.

Weeds are beginning to take over in the cemetery. Parents die and their children are living in the city or even abroad. A trip in November, for All Souls' Day, satisfies the conscience but does nothing to control the vegetation.

Luigi and I had shared a desk regularly in the single classroom of the elementary school. Years after our marriage I came across him working behind the counter of a post office not far from our house. It was May. We went for a coffee together to talk over old times and catch up with each other's news.

Driving past in your car, you saw us sitting side by side.

For many nights afterwards you prevented me from sleeping. 'Who was he? You have never smiled at me like that,' you kept shouting, hurling to the floor everything you could lay your hands on. Then you locked yourself into the sitting room and played Mahler at full blast.

I was already pregnant with Michele but you didn't know this.

Over the years I had come to know you. I had become as competent as a weather forecaster predicting typhoons. Almost always I could predict when they would blow up and what form they would take. Usually I took every precaution to avoid the most violent impact.

But even the experts sometimes get it wrong. I thought you had calmed down when I told you, 'I'm expecting another child.' You looked at me for what seemed like for ever. Then you hissed, 'Oh yes? And whose is it?' and punched me in the stomach.

Naturally, no one suspected the truth about our marriage. In public, on social occasions, you were the perfect husband, gallant, generous, in love with the beauty of your wife. When there were others present you would look at me with your eyes shining and say, 'Isn't she a jewel?'

When we were alone at home and you needed something, you called me 'Snow White'. When you knew I was expecting Michele, Snow White became Snow Whore.

The day I went into labour you were in the Far East on business. I went to the hospital alone, by taxi, leaving Laura with the baby-sitter. It was an extremely long labour. When the senior consultant came running I knew there was something wrong.

'What's happening?' he asked, palpating my stomach. 'What's going on?' There was a note of alarm in his voice. 'The baby's turned,' replied an assistant. 'The cord must be around its neck.'

At the last moment, Michele had decided not to be

born. Instead of his head he was presenting his feet to the world. Finding himself bound, he had tried to strangle himself. They pulled him out *in extremis*.

When they laid him on the table he was blue, as soft and lifeless as an old rag. 'He's not going to make it,' said one of the nurses. As the doctor tried to find a heartbeat, Michele breathed a sort of sigh and his little chest began to move.

It is difficult for anyone else to imagine what giving birth means to a woman, because every child is completely different. For some it is a cause of joy, for others only despair.

At that point in my life I was certain that, had Michele been born dead, I would have died soon afterwards. While, in a happy marriage, children are the natural extension of the relationship, when the union is undermined by problems they become life-lines to be grasped with all one's strength, small, defenceless beings to care for and which, in return for this care, day by day restore the damaged bond of love.

True, I already had Laura, but Laura was a girl and as she grew she had become more and more like you. Stubborn to the core, morbidly ingratiating whenever she wanted something, capable of violent outbursts of temper, Laura was your darling. Even before Michele was born I knew you would never treat him the same way.

He was in an incubator for nearly a month. When they brought him to me at last I felt as if I were holding a rag doll. He lay in my arms rolling his watery little eyes towards the ceiling with no resistance in his body, no inclination to move. When he suckled he often stopped, losing interest, as if prey to an ancient weariness.

You arrived after eight days. An enormous bouquet of red roses preceded you into my hospital room. When they left us alone you moved a chair close to the bed and took one of my hands in yours. 'I'm sorry,' you said. 'The child will never be normal.' The doctors had revealed to you what they had kept hidden from me. 'The brain', you continued, 'was starved of oxygen for too long.'

'So what of it?' I shouted.

You shrugged your shoulders. 'Nothing. We'll have another child.'

That day I learned that in every mother there is a little tiger. When he was three months old I took Michele to a famous neurologist in Milan. He examined the child at length, prodded him delicately, turned him this way and that as if he were a toadstool whose toxicity had still to be determined.

Then we sat down facing each other. Removing his glasses, he said, 'I don't like raising false hopes. It would be easier, but it wouldn't be right. So I shall tell you the truth. The child will never be capable of doing anything. I am almost certain that he is completely deaf and that his eyesight is minimal.'

'Is there nothing more you can tell me?'

'Think of a plant. If you feed it, it will grow, stretch out towards the light, breathe and synthesise chlorophyll, but you cannot expect it to talk or jump around.'

For the first time I went against your wishes. You wanted to shut him up in an institution for the severely handicapped, where our role as parents would be limited to visiting him at Christmas and patting his head. I wanted to keep him with me all the time, like a mother kangaroo, koala or opossum. I talked to him constantly and sniffed the warm puppy-soft skin. Meanwhile, you and I were fighting like cat and dog.

The day you referred to him as 'the little bastard' I threw a few things into a bag and went back to my mother. They knew nothing and treated him like a normal child.

It was here that he smiled for the first time and when his grandmother sang him a nursery song he burst out laughing.

A week later you came to fetch me. In one hand you were holding a bunch of flowers, in the other a package from a jeweller's. You wept before my mother like a man distraught. 'At times I can be rather short-tempered,' you told her, 'but I don't deserve such treatment. Besides, Laura can't sleep, she has nightmares and never stops asking for her mummy.'

That evening, when my mother and I were alone, she gave me a little lecture. 'In every marriage one is faced, from time to time, with some very steep stone steps. Looking at them, you think you'll never make it to the top. However, for your own sake and for that of the children, and because of the obligation you have undertaken, you have to find the strength to do it. And then, when you are old like me, you will look back and see not steps but only meadows full of flowers.'

The next day we left together, Michele in his baby-seat in the back, and the two of us in front. We smiled and waved as we left. I was still young; I wanted my mother to be right.

IV

Once, in some book or other, I read a story about a monkey and a scorpion. Reaching the bank of a great river, the monkey decides to swim across it. He has just put one paw in the water when he hears a tiny voice calling him. He looks around and sees a scorpion sitting nearby. 'Listen,' says the scorpion, 'would you be kind enough to give me a lift across the water?' The monkey looks him straight in the eye. 'I wouldn't dream of it. With that great sting of yours, you could attack me while I'm swimming and make me drown.' – 'Why would I do that?' replies the scorpion. 'If you drowned, I'd die too. Where would be the sense in that?' The monkey has a little think, then he says, 'Can you swear you won't do it?' – 'I swear it!' So the scorpion climbs on to the monkey's head and the monkey begins to swim towards the other side. When he is about half way across, he feels a sudden jab in his neck. The scorpion has stung him. 'Why did you do that?' the monkey screams. 'Now we'll both die!' – 'I'm sorry,' answers the scorpion, 'but I couldn't help myself. It's in my nature.'

What was your nature?

For so many years I tried to understand. I thought at first about some kind of trauma, some hurt deep in your subconscious that compelled you to act as you did. I was convinced that given time and self-denial on my part I could heal it and then, one day, we would achieve the banal normality of a family in a TV commercial.

Then, as the years passed, my energy began to flag and what little remained I exhausted on defending myself, so I no longer tried to understand. I knew by now that every word, every gesture, was a minefield. Any unnecessary adjective or misplaced adverb could result in a detonation. I moved cautiously, with the studied deliberation people adopt when there is serious illness in the house and all noise has to be avoided. Even the children learned to move in the same way. They were like two lemurs testing the strength of a branch before launching themselves into the void.

For weeks after your death I felt I was not alone in the house. Sitting on the sofa or crossing a room, I would feel a sudden icy draught. Although it was the height of summer I had to wear a woollen sweater.

Then one night, just before dropping off to sleep, I was sure I saw a shadow moving from the bathroom door to the bed just as you had done for so many years. The next day I went to stay with a friend.

'They don't even want him in hell,' I said, nursing a glass of whisky.

I no longer needed to defend myself. You had gone.

Slowly the desire to understand returned. I thought back over forty years of your life, forty years of which I knew, or thought I knew, every twist and turn, every breath you drew. During that time you had always succeeded in amazing me with your ability to mystify, your constant capacity for being pitiless, deceitful, for feeling nothing but the pleasure of humiliating others, a taste for trampling on their deepest, most intimate emotions. You seemed less of a human being than a destructive divinity like Shiva, perhaps, or a jellyfish with incredibly powerful tentacles. You spread poison all around you, and ink, too. Poison, to kill. Ink, to cover your traces so that you could gloat in secret over the despair you left behind you.

You were a successful man. You managed the company you inherited from your father better than most men could have done. Your employees respected you, those who worked closest to you thought the world of you. There were times when I had to defend myself against the envy of the other wives; they would have done anything to have a husband like you. You never dropped your guard in public. Over lunch you signed an important contract with your American partners; at suppertime, if I did not run to open the door for you, you shouted, 'Where's the alpine cow?'

For my birthday, the last we celebrated together, you gave me a pendant with a big black pearl.

'We're nearly over the hill,' you said. Then, raising your glass, you suggested a toast. 'To your death, which I hope will be more agonising than mine.'

You did not know it, but your sting had already done its work, injecting your poison into my body.

When he was four or five Michele was no different from other children of his age. End–of–term tests at school always showed him to be making excellent progress. The only remaining signs of his birth trauma were his physical weakness and a liking for quietude and silence. I wonder if a nudge from you lay behind the specialist's damning diagnosis.

To the same degree that you covertly despised him, he, at that age, adored you. The love withheld is always the love we long for most. Every evening, at the time you usually got home, he would stand by the door waiting for you. Whether he had to wait for ten minutes or a whole hour made no difference; he would be at his post. On the occasions when you dined out I had to use all my powers of persuasion to convince him that he was waiting in vain.

One day he set his heart on having a little tie. Children of his age had not been wearing ties for a long time and I had great difficulty finding one. In the end it materialised in a drawer at an old-fashioned haberdasher's. It was dark blue with red horizontal stripes and had a band of white elastic to go round the neck. Michele's eyes shone with joy. Back home, dressed like a little man, he stood very still in front of the mirror looking at himself, and then asked me, 'How many buttons of his jacket does Papa do up? Just one, or three?'

He wanted to be like the object of his love in every

way. So far I had managed to protect this vulnerable child; I did my utmost to avoid annoying you, to pre-empt your angry outbursts. If the worst happened I would close the doors and turn the radio up to full volume. I fooled myself into thinking I could keep his love for you alive, hoping that his dedicated devotion would, in time, make you feel differently towards him.

But you were unaware of him, of the effort he was making. Or if you noticed it at all, you did so with a sense of distaste. For you the neurologist's verdict had been final. Michele was mentally handicapped, not equipped for life. And even more importantly than this, in your morbid imagination he was a child who showed no sign of carrying your genes.

Educationally, you and I had had very different models. I had studied with the Montessori method while you were primarily influenced by Hobbes and Darwin.

'Life', you often used to say, 'is a driving force, and this force manifests itself in two ways, sex and struggle.' Without some going to the wall, without the diffusion of our genes, you maintained, life would have vanished soon after it first appeared. The fact that individuals are born with a varying capacity for dominance confirmed your thesis. Some were born to dominate and others to be dominated. To realise the truth of this you only had to look at the apes. In every group there was one male who was recognised by all the rest as the strongest, the leader, and he possessed all the females. The other males, apart from never so much as touching the females, would display their submission by presenting their backsides to him whenever he passed by.

And as for ourselves, you would say when in the mood of sober philosophising, in what way do we differ from them? We can talk, we can manipulate objects and work machines, but that's all. Deep down, in our wants and our sentiments, we are identical to them. Fuck or be fucked.

What a fool I was to expect you to appreciate Michele's delicate sensibility! You only saw him as a monkey incapable of swinging from one branch to the next. Unable to shake him out of the tree yourself – that was how handicapped individuals were dealt with in the wild – you simply waited for him to lose his grip while trying to jump. And while his mother shrieked in despair, you would have sat there with your arms folded and watched him fall.

Michele's blindness where you were concerned was cured just after he started school. The teacher had asked each child to do a picture to give his or her father on Father's Day, the Feast of St Joseph, and told them to write something nice on it. Michele was wild with excitement at the thought of handing you his picture. As soon as you sat down at the supper table, he came up to you and held it out with both hands, his eyes shining with happiness. He had filled the paper with irregular blotches of paint, all in pale colours shading harmoniously into each other. At the bottom of the page he had written in pencil, in capital letters: THREE CHEERS FOR DADDY.

'Oh, thank you!' you said, taking it. Then you turned it round and round, looking at it from all angles.

'But what is it? A house? A landscape? I can't make out anything at all. It looks like nothing more than a messy daub.'

Laying it on the table, you started to eat with your usual appetite. Michele sat on his chair, an untouched plate of spaghetti in front of him, while two little tears rolled down his cheeks. When you had finished your own plateful you noticed he had not started his.

'Eat up!' you shouted. 'Can't you see you're already a no-good wanker?'

With his eyes lowered he shook his head.

You repeated, 'Eat up!' three or four times. At the fifth, you jumped up, upsetting your glass; red wine spilled over the picture. With one hand you seized the fork, with the other you grasped him round the neck. Gasping for air, the child opened his mouth and you shoved the spaghetti down his throat.

After that day he never waited by the door for you again. Instead of asking me when you were due back, he ran and hid as soon as he heard your footsteps. The weaker, the more timorous he seemed, the more spiteful you became. 'A jelly,' you thundered. 'I have to give house-room to a jelly!' When you encountered him around the house, you said, 'Aren't you ashamed of yourself? You walk just like a girl.'

On one occasion Laura tried to defend him. 'What's wrong with walking like a girl?'

'I will not have you interfering!' you screamed at her, smashing your fist into the door.

Poor Laura! She did not have Michele's inner depths, but she did have the same kind of insecurity. She felt suspended between a mother who was incapable of defending her and a father who shouted most of the time.

As she grew up your behaviour towards her gradually changed. At first she was nothing but a silly little girl, then she started to become more interesting. When she was eleven, then twelve, you frequently praised her. Not for her schoolwork or character, but for her legs or her increasingly curvaceous behind. To begin with your remarks made her blush violently. She hid herself under baggy sweaters and looked like a survivor from a disaster zone. If she saw you staring at her she would leave the room immediately. Later, however, something in her began to understand. One had to live with love – no matter of what kind – or without it, to side with the weakest or the strongest.

So, at fourteen or fifteen, Laura made her choice. She chose to separate herself from her brother and me and to please you. She chose to use makeup and wear mini-skirts when her face and body still bore the traces of childish immaturity. She spoke to you as a woman would and you treated her as a woman. In the evening, after supper, the two of you would sit together in the sitting room, you in an armchair and she on your knee. You would exchange whispered conversations. I heard you laugh from time to time. When you wanted to smoke, she lit your cigarette. When you wanted a drink, she put the glass of whisky to your lips.

I have often seen women in talk shows weeping over their unhappy marriages and younger girls remarking acidly on their weakness. 'It's her fault,' they said. 'Why doesn't she leave him?' When things got really bad I too told myself that enough was enough, it was time to rescue what I could of my life. Then, once the anger had cooled, the humiliation worn off, I looked around and thought, where would I go? I had no training, nor income, nor property of my own into which I could move. My parents were poor mountain peasants and I still had two children to bring up. The law should have protected me but I knew that the law, in most cases, was a façade. It talks about the weak while protecting the strong, the cunning, those rich enough to afford the better lawyers.

To do anything like that would have taken much more nerve than I had. Those fifteen or sixteen years of marriage had left me broken-spirited, my capacity to react almost zero. And I was afraid. I knew that you would never tolerate the defeat of my leaving you, that you would be capable of anything in order to reassert your authority.

So I was a party, an almost helpless party, to my daughter's ruin. Only once did I say, 'Laura, I think we should have a talk . . .' She turned away with a toss of her head. 'There's nothing I want to say to you,' she replied, and left the room before I could say another word. She had chosen your side and could not bring herself to betray you. As your favourite, loyalty to you was her creed.

Michele, too, was growing up, and as he grew up he became increasingly solitary, increasingly thoughtful. He was doing well at school but had no friends; he spent whole afternoons without ever leaving his room. He loved reading, he loved drawing. He bore your insults as if they were a force of nature, never answering back, never raising his head.

Mothers often indulge in self-delusion, and I cherished some kind of hope where he was concerned. He's so lost in his own world, I told myself, that he doesn't notice how his father treats him. He didn't even confide in me to any great degree, but he was always gentle and affectionate. Every now and then, when we were at home alone, I would sit on his bed and ask him, 'What were you thinking?'

His invariable reply was, 'Nothing special.'

'Nothing?'

'Nothing. About life. About death.'

His pictures revealed phases of intense feeling. Over the first few years he loved painting the sky or the sea. He would take up his brush and wash blue all over the sheet of paper and then put spots of colour on top. Whenever I tried to guess what he was painting, he became impatient.

'Can't you see, they're stars!' Or, 'Look carefully! They're all fishes.'

At junior school, it was animals that he liked to paint. Not sparrows or squirrels but ferocious wild beasts were his only subjects. Big cats, jaguars, tigers, leopards. He always caught them in the split second before they pounced. There was intense concentration in those yellow-green eyes, those bunched muscles, a concentration about to explode with incredible force. It seemed impossible that these paintings were the work of a ten-year-old child.

I asked him once if I could frame one and hang it in the sitting room, but he gave a terrified start. 'No! No!' he kept saying with unusual determination, replacing the sheets in a folder with an elastic ribbon around it.

Later, the animal phase was replaced by that of the crosses. He drew big ones and little ones, scattered at random or in a geometrical pattern. All black, however. Very occasionally there would be some hint of landscape around. A leafless tree, a deserted house in the open countryside.

One day while he was at school I collected all his pictures together and took them to a psychologist. She pored over them for some time, holding her chin with one hand and every now and then asking me a question. The big cats and the seascapes were of no importance to me but I did want to know about the crosses. Were they a normal subject for a healthy boy of twelve?

The psychologist laid everything at the door of Michele's birth trauma. Those moments when he was hovering between life and death must, she said, have left an indelible mark on his personality. The child was probably unaware of what he was doing and was reproducing at random religious symbols learned in the family context. I objected that none of us was a believer and that, apart from being baptised, neither of my children had had any kind of religious education. She appeared to hesitate. After looking through the pictures again she hazarded an opinion. 'So maybe this is what he is trying to tell you. He feels he is missing something . . .'

A few months later Michele, for the first time ever, reacted to one of your bad-tempered outbursts. In his own way, naturally. We all knew how your rages progressed and could predict each stage. So a split second before the climax – flying china, kicks on the legs – Michele folded his napkin, murmured, 'Excuse me,' and left the room. You sat there frozen with astonishment. Then you glanced at me and ran after him.

He was not in his room nor anywhere in the house. He had gone out alone. Where could he be? To avoid giving you any satisfaction I feigned a calm that I was far from feeling, but as soon as you left for the office I threw myself into the search. I spent the whole afternoon scouring the neighbourhood. The longer I looked, the more terrifying the visions that assailed me. I thought of his ingenuousness, his grief, of all the dangers he could encounter.

I got home shortly before supper time. The house was in darkness. I switched on the light in the hallway, ready to phone round the hospitals, and saw him there, crouched in a corner. Thin and bony, he was holding his head in his hands and sobbing. I knelt down beside him. 'What happened to you, Michele?' I kept asking. 'What have they done to you?'

'Nothing,' he said without taking his hands away from his face. 'Nothing . . .'

'Then why are you crying?'

'I'm weeping for Jesus,' he answered, looking me in

the face at last. 'I weep because He died for our sins and no one understands.'

V

There is still a photo of Michele on the dresser here in the kitchen. It must have been taken at the time of his great change. He is with his grandfather in a field and, wielding a scythe bigger than himself, is helping him with the haymaking.

During that period this house had become his haven. He knew that with his grandparents he could be himself, he would be neither judged nor despised but would find only the affection of quiet people. You never worried about these holidays with my parents. When all was said and done it was one way of getting him out of your hair. But when you noticed that they made him happy you began to oppose them. Every time he planned a visit you invented some objection or put him in detention.

Happiness was like a poison for you, you could not bear to see it in other people's eyes.

Unbeknown to you or me, Michele had begun to take part in the youth activities of the local parish church. There was a young priest with whom he had struck up a warm friendship. After his fourteenth birthday, having said nothing about it at home, he made his first communion. I was the first to find out and I tried to conceal the fact for as long as possible. One day, however, on your way back from work, you saw him entering the church hall.

'Since when do you frequent such places?' you asked him at supper. 'Do you, by any chance, have my permission to do so?'

With the sudden bravura of adolescence he looked you straight in the eye. 'I have made my communion. Soon I shall be confirmed, too.'

For a moment I feared the worst was about to happen. Instead, you sat absolutely still, in perfect verbal and physical control.

'Is that so? I'm not surprised. What else could I have expected from a fool like you? Go and wear out your trousers on the pews, your knees on the floor. It's all you're good for anyway.'

Maybe because of his age, maybe because of his new companions, Michele was becoming stronger. For the first time in his life he had friends. He went on the occasional trip up to the mountains and spent afternoons collecting rags and paper. Instead of painting he sang. He had his own house keys now and I could hear him singing even before he opened the door. His voice was breaking. One moment it would be baritonal, the next it sounded like two pieces of broken glass rubbed together. Although it never grated on my ears, I was afraid it would annoy you. The false notes, the words would have irritated you, so would the pure light that radiated from his eyes. So ever so cautiously, making out that I was only joking, I said, 'Perhaps, until you've refined the tone, it would be better if your father didn't hear you!'

Michele was now nearly as tall as me. He was standing in front of the open fridge. He shrugged his shoulders. 'Too bad,' he replied. 'Nobody's ever died yet from a surfeit of false notes.'

Faced with the change in him, I found myself reacting ambivalently. Part of me was happy to see him opening up, while another part was frightened that people might take advantage of his vulnerability, force him into bad ways. With this in mind I would ask him from time to time, 'What company are you keeping these days? What do you do when you're all together?' His replies were uninformative. If I insisted, he said, 'Come with me if you're so curious.'

Once, when you were abroad, to keep him happy I went to Mass with him. He was extremely keen that I should hear his friend preach. On the way there he kept telling me, 'No one can hear him and remain indifferent. You'll see, it's like coming up against a wall. If you want to go on moving you have no choice but to change direction.'

We sat in one of the front pews. So many years had passed since the last time I entered a church that I could not remember any of the words. Not to disappoint Michele I moved my lips, pretending to pray. The lesson from the Gospels was the story about a treasure buried in a field. Michele was totally absorbed, but I had many things on my mind. I could find no clear reason for the change in him. The psychologist had put me on my guard. He is bound, she had said, to find some way of compensating for his weakness. For months I had lived with the nightmare prospect of drugs, alcohol or depression, but instead he had become religious. Everyone, I told myself, finds happiness where he can, whether it's supporting a football team or going to church every day. All the same, I was conscious of a slight sense of unease. Why? Was I afraid of losing him? Afraid he would make a choice I could not understand? Or was it subconscious envy, envy of his faith because it meant that everything in his world had its rightful place?

During the most difficult years I too had sought the sanctuary of religion. Passing a church, I would often enter and kneel at the foot of a statue. But the statue remained a statue. I would ask it, 'Who are you? Speak to me! Help me!' But the statue never responded. Kneeling before a stack of tins of tomatoes in the supermarket would have had exactly the same result. You always told me that religion and wheelchairs have much in common. Both serve the needs of those who cannot stand on their own two feet. In a wheelchair your movements are restricted; you can go backwards and forwards, left and right, but you cannot climb the stairs or rush headlong down a hill.

Naturally I said nothing about all this to Michele.

As we came out of the church he asked me, 'What did you think of it?' My reply could not have been more banal. 'Very interesting.'

Every now and then he would confide his thoughts to me. I must have been an indifferent liar because on one occasion he said, 'I can see you're not enthusiastic.'

'I listen to you willingly,' I replied, 'however, as you know, I have my own ideas and it would be difficult to change them.'

He leapt up angrily. 'Why are you so blind? Jesus is not an idea; he is the Saviour. Jesus is the beginning and end of everything. He is life and the key to the meaning of life.'

He left the room before I could answer.

It was the first time he had ever spoken to me like that. The cocoon of affection in which we had lived together for fifteen years had split.

Around this time I was summoned to the school. They wanted to know why his attendances were so rare. It pulled me up with a jerk. I saw him leave the house every morning with his satchel over his shoulder. It had never crossed my mind that he could be going anywhere else.

I returned to the psychologist. Religious obsession at this age, she told me, was not unusual. The hormones are becoming active and the libido is starting to get the upper hand. When this is repressed it can take a different direction from the usual one. And possibly, she added, his church-going provided him with a kind of safety valve for a latent form of homosexuality. She advised me not to give too much weight to the matter. If it was not allowed to become a problem, it would die down as quickly as it had blown up.

I followed her advice. To avoid making matters worse I kept everything to myself, but I did have a word with Michele.

'Why haven't you been going to school?'

'Because I get bored.'

At the end of June our secret was out. He failed his end-of-term exams.

'I always told you he was an idiot,' you remarked as you leafed through his report. Even given the courage to do so, this time I would not have known what to say. Then you turned to him. 'How much longer do you think I'm going to maintain you if you do nothing?'

Michele returned your gaze unflinchingly. 'You can stop now if you want.'

'Oh yes? And how are you going to live? Pimping?'

'I shall live like the lilies of the field.'

'Don't talk bullshit.'

'That's not bullshit, it's my faith.'

'Your what?'

'I believe in Jesus.'

You began to laugh loudly, then stopped suddenly. In a falsetto voice you chanted, 'I believe in Jesus! I believe in Jesus! Only a miserable poofter like you could fall for such rubbish!'

'I am not homosexual.'

'If you screwed like all the others you wouldn't get bitten by these crazes. No one with balls would believe in a cunt so pathetic that he let himself be killed.'

'Don't blaspheme.'

'I'm not blaspheming, my sweet, I'm telling it how it is. Jesus was a compulsive liar and also decidedly lacking in diplomacy. That's how he brought about his death. He thought too much of himself and got his calculations wrong.'

'Jesus is the Son of God.'

'Had he been the Son of God he would have come down from the cross and reduced the onlookers to ashes, even the Bible says so. He didn't come down because he couldn't.'

'He didn't come down because he chose not to.'

'He didn't come down because he was no more than a poor sucker who'd made up a pack of lies about himself. Things went wrong and he ended up being nailed to a cross.'

Michele stood up; he seemed taller than usual.

'You are the poor sucker!' he shouted, hurling the words in your face.

'Michele, that's enough!' I said, raising my voice.

But it was too late. With one slap in the face you sent his glasses flying, with the next you jerked his head back the other way.

'What did you say?' you said over and over, shaking him like a dry branch. 'What did you say?'

He remained silent, but his eyes never left yours.

'I'll teach you who's boss here! Lower your eyes!' you began to shout. The harder you shook him, the more steadily he met your eyes. So you dragged him to his bedroom. I do not know what happened in there. I heard your shouts grow louder and louder. He remained silent.

After an interval which I thought would never end, you came out locking the door behind you.

'He's in disgrace,' you said, slipping the key into your

pocket. 'And he will stay in his room until I decide to let him out.'

VI

How long did his imprisonment last? Ten days, perhaps fifteen. I had your permission to open the door three times a day. 'If you try anything on, I shall notice.'

You deluded yourself into thinking you could break him in this way. Every day you hoped he would beg you to let him out, but he stayed in his room with no sign of discontent, reading, writing up his diary. When you were not at home, he sang. It was the month of June.

At the beginning of July you went to visit your factory in Thailand, and as you left no instructions about the matter, I let him come out. I wanted to stay at home to be with Laura who was preparing for matriculation. When Michele asked if he could go to his grandparents for the haymaking, I said, 'Of course.'

He was no longer a little boy with his head in the clouds, but a young man with some clear ideas and a streak of determination that often left me bewildered.

While he was away he wrote me a letter, the first and last of his short life. I have read it so often that I know it by heart.

Dear Mamma, I went for a walk today up to the quarries at Ghiaioni del Comeglians. The air was cool and there wasn't a single cloud in the sky. Granny didn't like my going, but I put her heart at rest. I know the paths up there better than the streets of our own neighbourhood. Coming here makes me realise that I can't breathe in the city. It's all so ugly, so gloomy. The only sound and smell is that of exhausts. My heart is aware of nothing but the misery and loneliness of other hearts. Living separated from the natural world means living separated from beauty. And living separated from beauty means living separated from God. I know that when you read that last sentence you'll snort with disapproval. You think I'm like a cook who puts too much salt into every dish.

Rather than salt, I put God into everything and you don't like that. According to you God ought to stay in churches and the heads of priests. You said so yourself, do you remember? God is an idea. An idea like any other. I can believe in God or Che Guevara. I can even believe in nothing but Ferrari's F1 victories.

This is why you feel so alone. Sometimes you peer around you like a lost child. You may deceive yourself and other people, but you don't deceive me. I see the fear in your eyes. Your head is too full of ideas and deep down you don't know which is the right one.

But God is not an idea! He is the place from which we come and the place in which, one day, we shall be reunited. His is the tender compassion that guides us on our journey. Oh Mamma, how happy I would be if you could open your heart, surrender yourself like a newborn baby in His arms.

I always feel diminished in your presence. When I try to talk to you, you pick up my every word with a pair of tweezers, hold it up to the light and examine it as if trying to discover something hidden inside. Is there or isn't there a watermark? Is it genuine or is it a forgery?

In your heart you are convinced that my faith, for all its apparent serenity, conceals something else. A fear, some unresolved problem. Something that frightens me or that I refuse to face up to. Although you may not believe me, I can assure you that it is not so. Even as a small child I had a sense of great uneasiness. Perhaps that's why I never wanted to play with other children. What was this uneasiness? A feeling of suspense, of incompleteness. I was still conscious of the darkness I had only recently left behind me. I sensed that something similar awaited me. What was I doing here between the two? It was as if I had a crystal ball like a fortune-teller's inside me. But instead of being clear mine was opaque, muddied. Music, painting, choosing to be alone, these were only ways of trying to make it clearer. I knelt and rubbed it like Aladdin with his lamp. Ball, shine for me! And one day the ball lit up.

Only then I realised that it was not a ball, with a round solid surface, but a bud. Touched by the rays of the sun, the petals had opened. The bud had only been waiting for that caress before filling with light.

Then I realised that each of us carries this bud within us. Some bigger, some smaller, some more developed, some less, but always there. As soon as we let in a little light it begins to open.

That's why I take the liberty of asking why won't you think about the Light instead of ideas? You would never again have to defend, adjudge, discard or approve, but only surrender yourself, accept unreservedly that you are not the daughter of chaos and chance, but of the Light.

Poor Mamma! By now you will be bored rigid, having to put up with the sermonising of your own son. It's my fault because I can't resist the urge to share my joy with others.

I haven't told you yet what happened when I arrived at the quarry on the high slopes! I found a marmot suckling her babies. She was hiding under a big rock. Instead of running away when she saw me, she stayed there, quite still; her babies carried on suckling, and she looked me straight in the eyes. It was the first time I'd ever seen a marmot at such close quarters. Usually I hear their cries and glimpse their dark shapes scrambling back into the burrow. As you see, Papa is mistaken about this, too. According to him animals are too frightened to look a superior being in the eyes, but he's wrong. Perhaps it's true where baboons are concerned, but not marmots.

After picnicking under a little dwarf pine, I lay down and looked at the sky. How nice it would be if our lives could be as clear, as serene as that!

I keep thinking about that latest confrontation. Papa cannot bear the sight of me and never could because we are so different and he cannot understand me. I too get exasperated sometimes, because I try to cause him the least possible trouble, yet whatever I do he is always attacking me. I am beginning to think that the best solution would be for me to leave home quite soon. Meanwhile, I could stay here with the grandparents for the rest of the summer. What do you think? In the autumn I believe that I shall have an important decision to tell you about, and I need to feel strong enough to do it. Even if I give you both cause for concern in everyday life, I pray constantly for you and for your buds, that they may, sooner or later, accept the light and blossom into flowers. And I thank you with all my heart for having, in your generosity, brought me into this world.

A big, big hug nearly as strong as a boa constrictor's from your unfortunately once-docile son

Michele

The letter arrived the very day that you returned from Thailand.

'Where's your son?' you asked me. I told you the truth. 'He's gone to help his grandfather with the haymaking.'

You insisted that he should return home at all costs. 'He hasn't deserved any kind of holiday.'

I had to undertake long negotiations on the phone. Michele would not hear of coming back. Only when I said, in a voice that was close to tears, 'At least think about me, about how your father will make me suffer,' did he say, with a sigh, 'All right, I'll come.'

In the following months and years I've thought of nothing but that telephone conversation. I've gone over it again and again, taken it apart and put it together again. I've tried to remember all the pivotal points, the exact moment when fate, instead of moving forward, went into reverse. At length I had to realise that however I shuffled the cards the outcome was always the same. At the root of everything was simply and solely my cowardice. I should have had more faith in Michele, I should have stuck my neck out and stood up for him, I should have been less fearful of your violent reactions.

When Michele returned it was the end of July. The city was like a furnace, the streets were almost deserted and the tarmac oozed under one's feet. Laura had finished her exams. She had never been particularly brilliant at school and, true to form, had only just scraped a pass-mark. You were not critical in the slightest degree. 'A woman's fortune', you liked to say, 'certainly does not lie in her brain.' You had generously decided to give her a big party at home to celebrate both her eighteenth birthday and matriculation. With the company closed down for the holiday, you too stayed at home in her honour. As I went backwards and forwards with trays of canapés, I saw you always surrounded by groups of her friends. They were laughing at your jokes and you were caressing their thighs.

Michele arrived that evening. The music was blaring

out and the house was illuminated like a disco. He went straight to his sister and gave her a hug. 'You did it, huh?' They clung to each other for a while, saying nothing. Then she returned to the dancing and he threw himself down in an armchair.

He looked around him, smiling. I watched him for a second and had a feeling that he was somewhere else. Where was my son at that moment? Was he with us or somewhere else? I was baffled. At one point a friend of Laura's came and sat beside him, perching on an arm of the chair. They began to laugh and joke. You swooped like a falcon, grabbed him by the arm and jerked him to his feet.

'Is this your party?'

'No.'

'Then get out. You've got nothing to celebrate.'

I was afraid of how Michele might react. But he got up and left the room without a word.

I don't know why, but seeing him so docile made my heart ache. I wanted to run after him, speak to him, but it was impossible for me to leave the kitchen just then. I decided that I would go to his room as soon as you were asleep. I had been struck by his letter, which seemed a kind of life-line thrown across the abyss, something that would enable us to reconstruct the painful course of our two lives. I wanted to go to him and cuddle him as I used to do when he was little and would throw himself dead-weight into my arms.

But then I was overcome by exhaustion. You showed no signs of wanting to go to sleep, but moved around the room opening and closing drawers as if looking for something. My eyes, however, were closing.

'Not to worry,' I thought. 'Tomorrow's another day.' And drifted into my last sleep as a mother.

VII

Looking back on it I can see how it was, for me, like a photographer's flash. I was not ready and the flash blinded me. My life ended at that precise moment. The years I have lived through since then have been compressed into a fraction of a second.

You often read about presentiments in novels and magazines. Someone has a sudden intuition that something bad is about to happen, and then it really happens. I was aware of nothing that morning. On the contrary, I woke up in an unusually sunny mood. We were due to leave the next day on our annual sailing holiday with friends in Sardinia. I had the packing to do and lots of last-minute details to attend to. Michele, whose punishment had not yet run its course, was to stay at home and water the plants. That was his father's decision. He seemed perfectly content with it. Holidays by the sea had always been a torture for him. I went out early before it got too hot. You left shortly before me. Laura was still in bed. Asleep.

I did not see Michele during the morning but that was no cause for concern. He had always come and gone in his own mysterious way. We all had lunch together, finishing up the previous evening's leftovers. In the afternoon you went to your office to sort out a few things and I went out on a variety of errands.

We only met up again at supper time.

It was so hot that I opened all the windows to get some air into the room. Mosquitoes and little flies swarmed around the halogen lamp. Every now and then one of them hit the lamp and fried, giving off a little puff of smoke and filling the room with an acrid smell.

As usual, we waited for you before sitting down. To start without you showed a lack of respect that you would not have tolerated. Instead of arriving as you always did at eight o'clock, you arrived at ten past. Your face was very drawn.

Falling on to your chair as if your legs had given way, you said, 'Someone has stolen my money.'

'What do you mean?'

'I put it in the drawer and it is no longer there.'

I was about to suggest that some gypsy must have broken in when Michele said, 'It was me. But I didn't steal the money, I only borrowed it. You were not in so I couldn't tell you.'

You sat quite still. I could see the veins in your neck pulsing more rapidly than usual.

I broke the silence by saying, 'Michele, what were you thinking of?'

'I met somebody who needed it.'

When you spoke your voice seemed to be coming from somewhere deep down. It was almost a rattle. 'Who do you think you are, eh? Robin Hood? Robbing from the rich to give to the poor?'

'I've said I will give it back.'

'Oh yes? And how will you earn it?'

'I shall work.'

'You will work . . . And how do you think I earned it?'

'Certainly not by the sweat of your brow.'

Your arms began to tremble visibly.

'By whose sweat, then?'

Michele thought for a second or two. I wondered if he were afraid. I feared for him. He took a deep breath before replying, 'The sweat of the Asian children you exploit.'

At that point all hell broke loose.

Laura fled from the room. I tried, clumsily, to separate the two of you. 'Worm!' you shouted, hitting him. 'You also eat thanks to them, and buy your pansy clothes and go to school. Who do you think you are? Do you think you're different from me? Better than me? Tell me!'

'Different, yes. I believe in something.'

I heard myself say weakly, 'Stop it now, you'll kill him!' You thrust me back with a mighty shove.

'Ah yes, what do you believe in? Theft?'

Michele was now lying on the floor in a corner of the room.

'I believe in love.'

'Then go and screw.'

'In the love of the Spirit.'

Grabbing his vest, you yanked him to his feet. Beside his slight body you looked like an ogre.

'So', you roared at him, your face shoved close to his, 'turn the other cheek!'

With a childlike smile he responded with, 'Here it is!'

Focusing a picture on the screen with an old projector used to be a long process. At first you saw nothing, no faces, no background, only shifting blobs of light and colour. That is how I remember the hours leading up to the photographer's flash. I remember your slinging Michele out of the room. I remember hurling myself at you. 'You'll kill our son!' I shouted, while you grabbed my wrist. There was a tiger inside me and someone had set fire to its tail and driven it mad.

'He's got a heart of gold!'

'I don't give a toss for his heart!'

I don't know how long we raged at each other like

this, with no holds barred. I hardly knew what I was doing, time meant nothing, it could have been minutes or hours. Then the moment came when you hurled me against the hall table and went out, slamming the door behind you.

I heard you start up the car in the garage and the wheels crunch on the gravel driveway. You were revving the engine as young lads do when they're drunk. You slowed momentarily at the automatic gates. When they opened you accelerated away at top speed, tyres squealing.

I heard you brake suddenly. Then came a thud.

Thinking you had hit a dog, I looked out of the window. Michele lay on the asphalt as if asleep. One arm lay limply by his side and the other over his head as he used to lie in his cot as a child when it was too hot.

VIII

Hate is the one feeling that never evaporates with time. On the contrary, it continues to build up like a hurricane, a powerful, living force. It is hate that has kept me alive all these years, made me hard and stubborn, thirsting for vengeance.

I could have said that I live only for the memory of my son. But, being honest, I admit that I live only to avenge him.

Or rather, I lived in that expectation.

The expectation was thwarted once and for all the day I found you lying on the bathroom floor. I had hoped you would die in long-drawn-out agony. Cancer of the brain, some immunosuppressive illness that would leave you a skeletal wreck with incontinence pads. Instead of that, the good fortune that always protects the evildoers of this world saw that you died in the best possible way – a sudden heart attack – and left the other kind to me.

I had hoped that returning to my parents' home would lessen my pain, but I had not taken the silence and the memory of the dead into account.

Nor had I taken into account the fact that the oxygen-rich mountain air intensifies every emotion by stimulating the brain and the heart. As in olden times they used to burn a man's wife on his funeral pyre, so I collected the most precious objects from all over the house and piled them on my bed. In the evening I crawl under the mound and feel less alone, for these objects are still alive, they breathe, they emanate warmth. Even the pyjamas I wear are not mine but Michele's.

Wandering around the house the other night, I caught sight of myself in a mirror and noticed that I was radiating light. Was it me or was it someone standing near me? Was it the light of love or the light of hate? 'Who are you?' I whispered. A mouse, or possibly a dormouse, was pattering about on the ceiling above my head. 'Who's there?' I called out. A floorboard creaked; I had the impression that outside the wind was about to rise.

Tragic fatality, they wrote in the local paper next day.

Michele died instantaneously. You got out of the car and clutched your hair. You had not seen him, you could not have guessed that at the very moment you were driving through the gates at top speed he was running towards you.

I did nothing. I just stood there on the balcony, immobile, as if in a box at the theatre. I saw the ambulance arrive and the doctor shake his head.

An old white dog appeared beside the doctor. I noticed how it looked at you with its mouth gaping and its tongue hanging out, as if trying to tell you something.

I saw you seize the doctor by his lapels and heard him say, 'It's not our job now.' So you kicked the dog. Instead of whining and running off, it sat down slowly and painfully on the road beside the body.

I saw the police arrive and then the mortuary van. They put Michele into a plastic body-bag and then into a metal container. As they slid him in I heard a dull thump. That's his head, I thought. It's always been too big for his body since he was a baby.

I remembered the first jumper my mother knitted for him, pale blue with kittens embroidered on the front. The pattern was supposed to be for a child of six months, but I couldn't get it over his head and had to enlarge the neck by another couple of buttons. I saw again the top of the little blond head, the fontanelle still open, as I tried to pull it down and he protested. It was May, and we were staying with my parents. He'd just had a bath and was all warm and smelling of talcum powder.

When the doors of the van slammed shut, the spell was broken. I screamed 'Noooo!' as if there were no other word in the universe. Then I lost consciousness.

Throughout the funeral you held my arm in a tight clasp. I wept; you were as if turned to stone. I remember a sea of faces and some boys playing guitars. The August sun beat down upon us.

The priest who had been his friend perspired under his vestments.

'For some reason hidden from our small human minds, God often calls away His most spiritually gifted sons, abruptly curtailing their sojourn on this earth.'

Two tears ran down his cheeks and he made no effort to hide them.

'It would be easy to rebel, easy to resent an arbitrary act of such magnitude. Michele brought light into our lives and all of us, selfishly, would have wanted that light to last longer.'

The grandparents were standing in front of us. Just before the coffin was lowered they knelt beside it. His grandmother placed a light kiss on the lid. I saw her lips move as she said, very softly, 'Goodbye, little chick.' Grandfather was holding the little flute. He put it on the coffin with a timid caress.

Then there was nothing but darkness. Dark, dark, dark. Darkness with flashes of light. Darkness with lightning, thunder. Darkness with hail. Darkness with earthquakes and typhoons. Faces flashed before me, I heard voices. I saw your face saying, 'I shall still go sailing.' The face of a doctor saying, 'These will solve the problem.' The face of a priest. 'Go away!' I shouted. The face of my mother: 'Michele is still with us.' – 'Stupid liar!' I shouted. I was always shouting. Sometimes there were termites crawling over my body, getting into the most intimate crevices and devouring me with tiny jaws. At other times there were spiders, hordes of them, hairy, black, with short fat legs. They crawled all over me looking for the best place to inject their poison. At yet other times I felt sinuous snakes curling themselves around my ankles, flicking out their poisonous tongues. When I saw my face once again in a mirror, it was the face of an old woman. There are grandmother-wrinkles and witch-wrinkles. Mine were all witch-wrinkles.

After the tragedy Laura went to study abroad. She phoned me once a month with nothing to say.

You threw yourself into your work.

'It was an accident,' you kept saying. 'You killed him,' I would reply. And that was the sum total of our relationship.

I stayed with you in order to hate you to the end. But there was another reason. I stayed with you because I could not have survived a single hour alone with my grief.

How ingenuous I was to think I could defeat you on your home ground! I mentioned termites, spiders and poisonous asps, but not scorpions. You were the scorpion.

I still remember Laura's indignation one evening when we were watching television. They were showing a documentary about child prostitutes of the Third World. Your response was very laid-back, very much that of a grown man of the civilised world.

'You mustn't get too sentimental about it,' you said. 'Their life is very different from ours. They don't go to school, they don't read, they haven't got any food. At five years old they get raped by an uncle, at six they're on the streets. You see them around, you look them in the eyes and you realise immediately that there's nothing else they can do. That is their fate. And besides, they provide for their parents and their brothers and sisters.'

'Are you saying it's right?'

'No, only that it's hypocritical to overreact.'

Why didn't I slap your face? Why hadn't I done just that on many previous occasions? I don't know. Or perhaps I know only too well. Because I was afraid, because I was submissive, perhaps because in my heart of hearts I thought you were right. Because millions of people had blindly obeyed Stalin and Hitler and all the other dictators with never the shadow of a doubt about the rightness of their actions. You even told me once, 'I married you to reproduce myself, because you were beautiful and because you were healthy. I married you because you were poor and had no means of escaping.'

You didn't say, 'Because you were stupid,' but that was certainly in your mind.

Towards the end of my life, weakened by the devastating virus which has left me like an old hut riddled with woodworm, I realise that I could have made different decisions every day of my life. Every hour. Every minute. Every second.

It wouldn't have taken much. It would have been enough if I had had a little more confidence, if I had held my head just a little higher.

IX

The wind has been blowing for three days and has brought clouds. Summer is drawing to an end, the mountain-tops are dusted with snow. With the approach of autumn the scent of the earth changes. The sun no longer dries the morning dew, the fields stay damp. The leaves of the apple trees are turning yellow, the maples are turning red, the larches are ablaze. Log-stores are being replenished in preparation for winter. Any day now the cows will be brought down from the summer pastures.

Last week they brought Michele up here at last. I couldn't leave him down there in the city beside you. A little mound of earth beside the grave of his grandparents, near what will, quite soon now, be mine. I've planted marigolds on it, yellow and orange, like so many little suns. I hope they survive, that we won't have a frost yet awhile.

Some mothers, I've heard, manage to hear their children's voices on a tape recorder. They leave it running during the night and in the morning find loving messages on the tape. Others swear they have seen them in a crowd or found them appearing suddenly beside them surrounded by light. It has never happened to me. Michele has gone completely, he has not spoken to me, I have never seen him again. Perhaps I am too sceptical. Yet again I've been too timid.

The house is ready for winter. I've had the windows replaced, the chimney swept, the stoves cleaned. In place of the old wood-fired water-heater I've had an electric one installed.

The house is ready but my heart is not. I'm calmer now but far from at peace. Hate still bubbles up and spills over like dough with too much yeast in it.

I have not forgiven you and I will never forgive myself.

The earth is heavy under my feet and will be heavier still above me. I shall be a restless spirit, a ghost clanking round in chains, the first inhabitant of hell. Or the last. Or I shall be nothing at all.

Everything is rattling and banging tonight. It's terrible. I had forgotten that the north wind could come so close to hurricane force.

I've not slept right through the night for twenty years. Sometimes I lie quietly in bed, at others I wander around the house, drink a cup of milk, listen to broadcasts from faraway places. That's what happened last night. I got up, slipped on a heavy wool sweater and went to the kitchen. I couldn't stop thinking about hell, about the nonsense spouted by that theologian on television. So I got pen and paper and sat down to write a letter.

Dear Theologian whose name I do not recall . . .

Suddenly the lights went out and I had to get up and light a candle. Then I continued:

Some time ago I saw a programme of yours which left me feeling very angry. On one point I can agree with you. Hell is empty at present because all the devils, of every rank, are running about the earth. I'm not an ignoramus nor a medievalist. I say this because I shared my life with one of them. Every day I see how degraded humanity has become and realise that it could not have achieved this alone. The devil does not stink nor is he a primitive. His pre-eminent quality is skill. He knows the human soul better than most and can insinuate himself into anyone's skin. He does not use foul language nor utter obscenities, but uses rational, refined arguments. 'Don't you think you deserve more out of life, much more?' he asked me many years ago, and I thought he was right, that I should no longer be satisfied with so little. He does not expose himself indecently nor does he fart, but escorts us into the maze of life with the light grace of a dancer.

Hell is empty only because the master of the house has gone to fill his hunter's pouch in the world of the living. Soon he will return to the underworld bowed by the weight of his prey. Everyone will be howling, clamouring, trying to rebel. 'Was this how it was supposed to end? Why did no one tell us?' But it will be too late.

Somewhere I read that long ago painters showed the men who were close to God with long ears because they heard His word at first hand. Now, however, we live in a world of moles. We are blind, and our outer ears are all but invisible. I have tried many times to hear some voice from above but unfortunately have heard nothing.

But I have heard plenty of noise from down below.

I would like to believe in the faith, to have everything sorted out before I depart this life, but I cannot. I have seen evil spread unchecked across the face of the earth. It has darkened my life and that of those close to me like an ink-stain. Injustice, inequality and violence. They and only they are the laws that govern the earth. Which is why I say this to you: Leave us the joy of hell at least. Hell crowded and noisy as a beach in August. I cannot wait to sink into it and suffer for evermore. Because in my life I have provoked nothing but sorrow and it is just that I should live in sorrow for ever.

One last thing. You also said that we should love the devil because the devil lives alone with his despair.

But I tell you that we can forget about the devil's tears in the same way that we can forget about the crocodile's.

Regards.

And I scribbled my signature illegibly at the end.

It was nearly five o'clock and still dark. The power had not come back. With the candle in my hand I went to look for an envelope. There were several in the drawer under the telephone. I picked up a white one and found it was lying on top of an old, yellowing sheet of folded paper with Michele's writing on it.

Night in the summer pasture. Stars watch over the rocks and the woods. But their gaze is cold. Sense of solitude. Where am I going? The darkness amplifies questions, puts them beyond reach. I breathe again only when the first faint streaks of dawn appear.

Lord, how great is Thy mystery! To give us light, you created darkness. To give us life, you created death.

As I was reading these words, a gust of wind nearly tore one of the windows off its hinges. It roared in, sending sheets of paper and ashes from the fire flying all over the room and overturning my mother's workbox. In it were all the leftover wools from the jumpers she had knitted for us in the course of her life. Jumpers for Laura, Michele, me, my father. I could still tell perfectly well which colours belonged to which jumpers. Swept along by that invisible hand the balls of wool began to roll all over the floor. I crawled about trying to gather them up.

The first I picked up was pale blue.

At that precise moment the candle blew out and a shaft of white light darted across the room.

The Burning Wood

I

I KNOW HER AGE but not her face. That is why I can't sleep at night. She was born on the third of March at three in the morning. The third hour of the third month, 1983.

A friend versed in the esoteric was impressed. Not many people, he said, are born with such perfect numbers. It meant little to me. Giulia was slightly underweight and, like all newborn babies, really rather unappealing.

She spent the first few days in an incubator. A touch of jaundice, nothing more, but it was enough to open the floodgates of her mother's anxiety.

'They're keeping something from me,' she repeated constantly like one possessed. 'There's something I'm not allowed to know.'

So I sat on the bed for hours trying to reassure her, even though I knew it was completely useless.

When they put the baby in her arms at last, she looked at it as one looks at an article one has just bought and suspects of being damaged.

'She's not taking enough milk,' she said. 'Is she or isn't she breathing? I don't understand.'

Eventually she succeeded in infecting me with her

suspicions. I buttonholed the consultant in the corridor one afternoon.

'What is wrong with my daughter?'

We were standing in front of the window giving on to the nursery.

Giulia was sleeping on her tummy in a cot right under the light. Judging by the faces she was making, she was probably dreaming.

'Why do you think there's anything wrong with her? Look at her,' he said, smiling. 'She's a little flower just waiting to grow.'

We went home the next day. Anna, outwardly at least, was calm. But the change of surroundings upset Giulia. She turned day into night and night into day. She yelled as if she were hungry but, as soon as Anna offered her the breast, turned her head away. Only after considerable persistence could she be persuaded to suckle. The struggle was exhausting. Once she had put Giulia back in her cot, Anna burst into sobs.

'She doesn't like me,' she cried. 'She doesn't want to have anything to do with me.'

With the paediatrician's agreement we changed to bottle-feeding after a week. In Giulia's case the improvement was immediate, but not in Anna's. Giving birth had caused a latent depression of long standing to re-surface. She no longer washed herself, shopped or cooked. I would get home from work in the evening to find the baby bawling with hunger and up to her neck in filth.

In no time at all I had to learn how to do all the things mothers do: changing nappies, applying talcum powder, testing the temperature of the milk with my lips.

The girls at my old grammar school used to say I was the best of the bunch. The boys in the class insinuated that I was gay, but they were wrong. I simply preferred reading to playing football. If I went out with a girl I liked talking to her rather than canoodling.

Perhaps this is why I wasn't too disturbed when I found myself cast in the role of mother. Instead of going out drinking with my friends, I accepted my responsibilities. It takes two to make a baby, I told myself repeatedly. If one partner is incapacitated, it is right that the other should take over. One day, I thought, she will be well again and my sacrifice will have served to create a happy family.

I loved Anna more than anything else in the world. I loved her vulnerability, her unpredictability. Above all I loved the fact that she could not live without my love.

I had met her at school when she joined my class in the penultimate year, her family having just moved from another town. She sat in the third row and hardly ever said a word. While the other girls did all they could to attract attention, she did all she could to avoid it. Reserved, quietly dressed, if asked a question she would blush before replying. Naturally, she became an object of some ridicule. The girls decided she was either stupid or had something to hide. The boys shrugged their shoulders and said she wasn't worth bothering about, she was convent-fodder and flat as a pancake anyway.

One afternoon I happened to meet her in the park. It was May, the swans were gliding over the pond with outstretched necks while the sparrows took dust-baths. We talked about school, about the teachers we liked or didn't like, about the coming exams, the holidays and what we intended to do in life.

'Have you got any special interests?' I asked her at one point.

'Special interests?' she repeated, lowering her eyes. 'Yes, I like reading. Poetry, novels . . . I mean, I'd like to study literature. But I haven't made my mind up yet because I'd also like to study psychology. So much goes on inside our heads, it would be nice to understand something about it, don't you think?'

'Oh indeed,' I replied. Then I told her about my passion for trees. I intended to study either biology or agriculture.

She looked astonished. Perhaps she was wondering how anyone could be interested in anything as boring as trees.

'Even trees', I told her, 'can be nice or nasty. Have you ever thought about that? For example, see that Arizona cypress over there? What do you think of it?'

Anna looked at it for a few moments, then pulled a face. 'Nasty.'

'And that?' I pointed to a weeping willow.

'Nice. Very nice.'

I suddenly found myself thinking that I could even fall in love with a girl like this.

Then came the prolonged panic of exams and the relief of passing them, followed by a short holiday before starting the process of enrolment at a university. So I lost sight of her.

I met her again a few months before graduating. She came up to me in the railway booking office and asked, 'Do you remember me?'

We went off for a drink.

'So how do you feel about that one?' she asked, pointing to the branches overhead.

'It's a Japanese zelkova,' I replied. 'Nasty, very nasty.'

We were married a year later.

Over this long period I have written many times to Giulia. I began four years ago by sending her a Christmas card and then a birthday card. On the first occasion I sat for a long time with my pen poised. How should I sign the card? Papa? Your father? Saverio? Or even, your papa Saverio? I couldn't decide. I opened and closed the envelope so many times that it looked old and tatty before I posted it.

The following year I screwed up my courage and wrote the first letter. I chose paper I thought would appeal to a girl of her age, decorated with a picture of kittens chasing a butterfly. Writing it took over a month; it was like carving words on stone. Then I let it sit on a table for another month. After posting it I waited for a reply. The days were distinguished one from the other only by the level of anxiety. Will it or won't it arrive?

Eventually a letter did arrive. But it was mine, returned to me. The envelope bore the message 'Addressee unknown' stamped in red ink. I had sent the cards to the same address. What had gone wrong? Perhaps something had happened to the grandparents. Perhaps they were ill or even dead. Or perhaps she herself was ill. I couldn't stop worrying. They had lived in the same house for generations, was it possible they had suddenly moved away? Or perhaps the truth was that the grandparents had refused to allow her to receive my cards. They had put them back in the red mailbox like throwing an underweight fish back in the water.

Go back. Go back to where you came from.

Much of my time is spent watching television. I watch mostly programmes for young people, wondering if she prefers this one or that one. Is she a fan of some singer or would she rather be in the garden, looking after the plants? Is she the apple of her grandparents' eyes, or a thorn in their side?

At night I often dream about her. I find myself walking along a street in a big city like New York or Los Angeles.

I see her in the crowd. She's walking some way in front of me, I call her but she doesn't hear. So I run after her and when I eventually tap her on the shoulder, she turns round and I don't recognise her. 'I'm sorry,' I stammer. The banal dream of a banal person.

In the days following the crime, they sought out some of my old schoolmates. They wanted to know what sort of person I was. Some had difficulty remembering me at all.

'Saverio?' they repeated, in the manner of a person rummaging in a trunk for some object of little value, and then, 'Oh yes, an ordinary guy, a very ordinary guy. Who would ever have thought it?'

I try to think of something else, but fail. The face I remember is that of a four-year-old. She was losing the chubbiness of babyhood and Anna tied her hair into two little pigtails before taking her to nursery school. She hummed as she went out of the door carrying her pink plastic lunch-basket. She is a part of me still out in the wide world, still looking around her, being surprised. Does she know the truth? Or not? I do not know and I am not allowed to know. For many years I have been thinking about disappearing from her life. For many years I have been thinking of suicide.

I think about Giulia, not Anna. Why? Because Anna is living with me again.

There came a point when she returned and I, instead of pushing her away, welcomed her back. It wasn't easy. It didn't happen at once. At first I didn't want to see her, then I was frightened. She spoke to me and I could not believe the things she told me. I felt insecure, confused. So I requested a session with the psychologist. After meeting him my thoughts were even less clear than before. So I proceeded to the psychiatrist, who gave me

132

drugs. They made my tongue swell, but she was still there.

'Listen to me, Saverio,' she said in a soft, gentle voice. I screamed, ran, threw myself against all four walls in turn. I felt as if someone had set fire to me, as if a tape recorder had turned itself on inside me.

'Even you want to kill me!' I shouted at her one night, waking up in the dark.

The mistral was blowing hard. Dawn could not have been far off because I could hear the fishing boats returning to harbour. Her voice was a gentle rustling.

'No,' she replied, 'I want you to start living.'

II

Seagulls keep to a strict schedule. At dawn small groups of them fly over the sea to the mainland. Shortly before sunset they return. They spend the daylight hours on refuse tips feeding on filth.

When we lived in town I often used to see them squabbling over scraps of rubbish. They were more like chickens in a chicken run than seagulls. What had happened to the noble creatures from which poets had drawn inspiration from time immemorial? Those birds were stupid, graceless, greedy. Impossible to imagine they could be the same species as these majestic, solemn birds gliding over the sea to their roosts at dusk.

Which is the real seagull? The snowy, solitary sea-creature or the feathered bully of the gutter?

And if birds, lacking a conscience, can be so ambivalent, what about us?

What arrogance to thump our breasts crying 'This is me'! Who am I? I cannot tell. All I can possibly know is how I appear. How I appear to myself, how I appear to others.

For many, this is enough. We are but bit players, we should be happy with our lot. But there comes a time when even a bit player can rebel. Any actor can become bored if he has to repeat the same insignificant role night after night, perform the same bow, speak the same line. Then out of the blue, without knowing who or what provided the spur, he starts tearing at his costume, rolling in excrement and shouting obscenities.

Who spoke to me? Was I following orders, or acting on my own volition?

I have never believed in the soul, but certainly in DNA. Invisible to the naked eye, it is nonetheless tens of kilometres long and lasts for hundreds, thousands, millions of years. This is enough to make any claim to knowledge ridiculous.

Without knowing it, any one of us might have a cut-throat for a distant ancestor. One who did it not as a job but for pleasure, who, as soon as he took a dislike to someone, would leap on him and carve a wide smile under his chin. The descendant of this distant ancestor shaves every day and when he sees a pedestrian waiting at a crossing, slows down, stops and with a courteous gesture lets him cross the road. Attending a parents' meeting at school, he tones down his sharpest criticisms and his reasonableness helps everyone find the best solution.

But suddenly that gene that has slept for centuries wakes up and the descendant, rather than intervening to calm a quarrel, cuts the combatants' throats. Howls of horror, of astonishment. How can this be? Who would ever have thought it! Such an honest, sweet person!

The night, the long, long night passes. A night that seems

never-ending, like the nights of the very sick. You long for dawn, you wait for it, but in vain. So you start asking yourself questions such as: where does that particular gene come from? Was it essential for the process of evolution? In the animal world murder within the same species is relatively rare, among humans it is almost the norm. We eat, we drink, we reproduce and we kill our fellow-men. This is the song-sheet from which we all sing. So, I ask myself, where did it come from? Abel was good but Cain was not. But even Cain seemed good to begin with. He ploughed the earth and fed the animals just like his brother. Suddenly, something happened and he changed. Why?

If hate defies definition, how can we define love? Any words we use run the risk of being mawkish. All I can say is this. There has never been a day, an hour, a minute in which my thoughts were not focused on Anna. Waking up, I thought of her. Driving the car, I thought of her. Working, I thought of her. Thinking, I wondered how I could make her life easier. I knew that without me she would have been lost. Her life shed light on mine, gave it reason and direction.

When Giulia was one year old things began to improve. Giulia was precociously bright and had a happy disposition, which reassured her mother to some extent. When she took the baby out in the pushchair, everyone stopped her and said how sweet, how pretty she was. Anna felt proud to be her mother. She was still consumed by anxiety, but managed to keep it in check with drugs.

And as time passed I learned about her, as a show dog learns about the obstacles he has to negotiate in the ring. Three marking-stakes over there, a slide to the right of them, beyond that a corrugated-iron tunnel and then a tyre to jump through. A five-minute delay getting home meant I would find her in tears on the sofa, convinced I was lying injured in the road. Forgetting to do or buy something she had asked for implied total desertion.

When I was out working for the whole day I called her from every public telephone available, every isolated booth at a crossroads. When I had an assistant with me, I invented excuses for phoning her every other minute. My mother was ill, I said, or something of the kind.

I was jealously protective of our mutual dependence. I knew that, seen from the outside, it could have elicited not the kindest of comments. Few people, I told myself, are lucky enough to be blessed with such an intensely loving relationship, so the wisest course is to keep it secret. I heard my colleagues' stories about continual quarrels, vindictiveness, restless wives who only waited for their husbands to leave the house before slipping out to enjoy themselves.

Once I even had a slight argument with one of these men. 'Don't you ever get bored with your wife?' he had asked jokingly.

'Only someone ignorant of the meaning of love could say something like that,' I retorted.

I knew our acquaintances called us 'the love-sick parrots' but I shrugged it off. They're only bitter, I told myself, because they're envious.

At the time I was working for an environmental protection association; my job was to deal with the diseases affecting trees. I was putting my expert knowledge to good use and this gave me a feeling of satisfaction.

Sometimes at night I close my eyes and can't sleep. I see fire. A fire that is not a fire. It's a forest of larches. It looks like autumn, but it cannot be autumn because the grass is tall in the surrounding pastures. Yet again, appearance and reality are at odds. Someone is walking under the trees and that someone is myself. The woodland is the woodland for which I am responsible. At the beginning, it is still green. There is only a suspicion that defoliating caterpillars might be at work. I collect a few leaves, some bark, place a few pheromone traps that will tell me if the adult moths are present.

Meanwhile, at home, Giulia has fallen out of her high chair and has a huge bump on her head. There are no phones in the wood, so I know nothing about it. I hear about it only on my way home. When I enter the flat, Giulia is on the sofa with Anna holding her tightly. She is crying.

'It's my fault; she can't see out of one eye.'

Markers, tunnels. Useless trying to reassure her, to tell her that all children, sooner or later, fall out of their high chairs.

Early next morning I take them to the hospital. From there I phone my colleagues to tell them I shall be in a little late. But the doctor walks out of the emergency room with Anna looking like a ghost beside him. I hear him say, 'I want her admitted immediately.'

That same day, the moths arrive in the wood.

A wood usually dies more slowly than a man. It can take months or even years. But once it is dead it is dead. And with it all the other life-forms die too. Lichens and mosses, beetles and red ants, weevils and crossbills, goldfinches and long-tailed tits. Everything that can, escapes. Everything that cannot escape dies with the wood.

My death and the death of the wood began with a curious simultaneity.

Giulia had injured her head in some way but the doctors were not sure what was wrong. They would have to operate to find out. Walking on the first of the fallen needles, I was worried not about Giulia but about Anna. If Giulia dies, I told myself, that's fate, but how could Anna survive? As I walked I suddenly felt the frailty of my shoulders. How many burdens were piling up on them?

Spending every day at the hospital, Anna was becoming paler and paler and her voice had dwindled to an echo of its normal self. As often as possible I would hold her tightly and speak softly into her ear.

Because they had shaved Giulia's head, her eyes looked enormous and the sparkle had left them.

Although the operation had gone well and she was making good progress I should still have been feeling worried, even desperate. But instead I felt like a lion. My energy levels were extraordinarily high. I was the linchpin, I could not collapse.

We had to wait for the results of the biopsy. A few days before these came through, Anna and Giulia came home.

In the wood the first two trees had turned yellow. If you ran your hand along a branch needles fell like rain. Needles falling in the wrong season affect one more than leaves. They fall like teeth. Leaves float gently down, needles just drop. A black, leafless branch is like a toothless gum. Everything around it is alive, but it is dead. Or nearly.

In hospital Anna had become friendly with one of the nurses. On several occasions I had seen them talking earnestly with their heads close together.

Returning from the wood one evening I found the flat empty. As we were expecting the results the following day, this was worrying.

I spent the whole night driving around in the car. I checked the river and the bridges several times. Anna could have done something silly. What appeared to us as silly could have seemed quite natural to her.

As soon as it was light I went to the carabinieri and reported her as missing.

Shortly before midday I heard her key in the lock. She was carrying Giulia and smiling. Kissing me as if she had just returned from a day out, she went to pick up the phone.

'What are you doing?' I asked.

'Calling the consultant.'

'I'll do that!'

She shrugged her shoulders. 'No, you needn't bother.'

After a minute the reply came. Anna dropped to her knees, still clutching the phone.

'Papa, I want a dwink of water!' shouted Giulia.

'So?' I shouted, so loudly that it frightened the child and she burst into tears.

'So?'

Trembling, Anna covered her face with her hands saying over and over, 'Thank you God! Thank you God! . . .'

Finally I grabbed her shoulder.

'Do you only speak to God,' I shouted at her, 'or will you condescend to speak to your husband?'

III

Fire never breaks out on the island. Too much rock, too little vegetation. Although fires never break out, I can always smell fire. But what is the smell of fire when there is nothing burning? Burning wood smells different from burning blankets. Burning feathers and bones smell different from burning leaves.

At night I dream of larches transformed into flames. Each tree is a single sheet of flame. Looking closer, I see they are not trees but people. Or rather, larches with human heads. I see Anna's face up there, and Giulia's, and mine too. We all blaze without a whimper, without an oath. There is only the dry crackle of dead branches. And I pace around under them, my hands in my hair, repeating, 'They were caterpillars, not flames! Why is everything burning? I have never believed in hell!'

The first time she came it was at night. I felt something cool on my cheeks, opened my eyes and saw her eyes shining at me. There was a tremendous sadness in them. Something, or someone, I don't know which, breathed, 'What have you done?'

I have never believed in hell, devils or even ghosts, and in consequence I have never believed in God either. On the contrary, I have always found the very idea of God distasteful. Why do we need to drag him in to account for the universe when we have the laws of physics and chemistry? Everything can be explained by their interaction.

After Giulia's illness Anna became a different person.

She often went out with her new friend the nurse and came home laden with packages. She began to take an interest in her appearance, to use a little light makeup and wear livelier, more colourful clothes.

One day I got home to find vases of primroses on every windowsill. Without even greeting her, I rounded on her.

'What are you thinking of?'

'I thought you'd like them. It is spring, after all.'

'Maybe, but these flowers should be left in the woods, don't you know that? You could have told me you wanted to see primroses and I would have taken you to see them. But to put them up here, surrounded by all this concrete, like little decapitated heads . . . Oh no. They turn my stomach.' And so saying I began to tear them to pieces and throw them on the floor.

Seagulls do the same. When they quarrel they tear the grass with their beaks and toss it on the ground nearby as if to say, watch out, next time it could be you instead of the grass.

I was now phoning her every half-hour, but she was never in. In the evening I would mention carelessly, 'I tried to call you at four o'clock but you weren't around . . .' She was always calm. 'I went out with Silvia,' she would say. 'We took Giulia to the park . . .'

They often went to visit some monk in a monastery on the outskirts of town. Anna's eyes shone when she talked about him. 'You should meet him,' she kept saying. 'He's an extraordinary man.'

'As you know,' I would reply, 'such things do not appeal to me. What difference does it make if God exists or not?'

'It makes all the difference!'

I had never known Anna to speak with such vehemence.

'Think of a flower,' she said. 'It's one thing to see it as a flower. It's blue or yellow or red or purple. It has petals and sepals, an ovary, a stem, a pistil. It can grow in the fields or cling to rocks. It's quite another thing to see it as the fulfilment of a dream. Someone has imagined beauty for us and has translated it into reality by creating the flower. A flower is first and foremost a gift to our sense of sight.'

'Who has taught you to think in such a muddled way?'

'It seems quite clear to me,' she said, lowering her eyes.

In the morning, I once heard her singing while she was getting breakfast. So I shouted from the bathroom, 'Turn off the radio!'

Where had my Anna got to? Where was the vulnerable creature who had dominated my thoughts for years? We now saw each other first thing in the morning and then no more until the evening. During the day we were strangers.

Because the dodging of markers and tunnels was now a thing of the past, I too had begun to have my own life. I spent more time with my colleagues after work, went into town for a drink. Sometimes I got home to find the table still unlaid.

A work-mate had once said to me, 'Why can't you see what's staring you in the face? When a woman changes, there's only ever one reason for it. Someone else has come into her life. She's buying new clothes, using makeup, singing. Surely you're not stupid enough to think she's doing it because of something an old monk said to her!'

In the Gospel story, the Devil climbs the mountain and says to Jesus, 'All this will be yours if you obey me.' You could compare the Devil to an estate agent or a clothes moth. Or even to a seed of one of those burrowing grasses like brome-grass for example, that clings to the body and crawls where it will, creeping under the skin like a tiny, silent arrow. Unseen, unheard, it burrows away. It knows perfectly well where it is going. It climbs up to the brain or down to the heart. And once there it explodes, it germinates.

So those words had been burrowing words. As I stood there they began to claw their way ever deeper. How could I not have thought of it before? The friendly nurse, the monk, the continual expeditions ... Clearly there was only one explanation. Throughout the years when our love was a living force, her eyes had never shone like that.

With the thread of suspicion one can stitch any garment. And so it was that, piece by piece, I slowly reconstructed the sequence of events. A name and a face came into focus. Who else could it be but the consultant? He had been so supportive through all those days of suspense and uncertainty. Giulia's fate had been in his hands. No negligence, no carelessness had marred the operation, everything had gone perfectly.

This was not for the child's sake, obviously, but to milk the last drop of admiration for himself. He had seen the desperate young mother as a plum ripe for the picking. All he had to do was stretch out his hand and help himself. Nothing better than a woman in need of consolation, of reassurance. Indeed, the pig had chosen his career with just that in mind. Distressed mothers fell into his arms one after the other. And it was obvious that the nurse, Silvia, acted more or less as his go-between. She identified the victims. She went out with them, talked to them constantly about him in order to increase their hero-worship.

The ultimate proof had been the telephone call for the results. Anna had picked up the phone and dialled the number from memory. Every movement spoke of familiarity, an easiness astonishing in someone usually too timid to phone down to the corner shop in the block!

And the monk, what could he be if not a code-name for some motel on the outskirts of town?

I walked through the wood obsessed with these thoughts. I had no companion with whom I could let off steam, so the seething anger began to bubble up uncontrollably. I talked aloud to myself as I walked. I kicked out at anything within reach. Dead needles rained down on my head, my shoulders. The only thing that brought a temporary easing was the idea of revenge. I thought of all the ways in which I could harm them. I felt my brain creaking with the intensity of my imagination. I clenched my teeth hard as if cracking a bone between my jaws. I could tell his wife everything, send her an anonymous letter using print cut out of a newspaper. I could write insulting graffiti all over his elegant car. I could lie in wait for him outside his house and teach him a lesson.

I could no longer hide my agitation from Anna. At night, beside her, I tossed and turned.

One night I reached the end of my tether. When she asked me, 'What's the matter? Why can't you sleep?' I answered, 'You smell different.'

She burst out laughing. The laughter sounded carefree. 'I'm using a different moisturiser!'

'Couldn't you think up any better excuse?' I muttered before climbing out of bed and going to the sitting room to sleep.

She came and sat beside me on the sofa. She looked at me anxiously.

'Don't touch me,' I said. 'You disgust me.'

She touched me all the same.

'Saverio, what's going on?'

'What's going on is that you've changed.'

'True, but why should that make you angry?'

'Because when a woman changes there's only one reason for it.'

'And what's that?'

'Do you really want me to spell it out to you?'

'Yes.'

'She's in love with another man.'

Anna sighed deeply. 'It's true that I'm in love, but not with another man.'

'With whom, then?'

'I'm in love with life itself.'

'Don't give me that women's-magazine bullshit.'

'It's not bullshit. That's how I feel.'

'Have you gone off your rocker?'

'No, I've found a reason for living.'

'But you already had a reason. Me, us, your family.'

'You still are. More than before.'

A laugh like a howl rose from my throat.

'I'd never have known it! "Darling, I shall be late this evening. Darling, haven't they done my hair nicely! What nice perfume I'm wearing! Look how well I can wiggle my hips with these new heels! Look, darling, look! Aren't I the very picture of a whore?"'

Anna stood up. I kept my back turned to her.

'Why must you hurt me like this?'

'Because I see the truth.'

'You see nothing but figments of your own imagination.'

'As we're on the subject, why don't you take me to meet your famous monk?'

'I didn't think you'd be interested.'

'On the contrary, I'm exceedingly interested.'

I fell asleep on the sofa laughing. She had painted herself into a corner. Lies have short legs. Was there ever a truer saying?

She took her time to set the scene properly. A week went by before she said, 'They're expecting us at the monastery at four o'clock this afternoon.'

We drove Giulia to a birthday party at the home of one of her nursery-school friends, then headed for the ring road. Anna was driving and not a word was said during the entire journey. It seemed to me that she swallowed hard every now and then like an animal when it senses danger.

The monastery was a collection of ugly buildings about twenty miles outside town. It was surrounded by the featureless uniformity of single-crop fields interrupted by the occasional row of leafless poplars.

The entrance was cold and gloomy. The brother who opened the door showed us to two small fawn leatherette armchairs and invited us to sit down. Then a door at the end of the passage opened and an old man appeared. Anna rose and went towards him.

I saw them embrace, and saw him take her hand between his with a gesture of affectionate intimacy. I remained seated. Standing in front of me, Anna said, 'Saverio, my husband.'

The monk shook my hand and invited me into a small side room.

We sat facing each other. I was looking at his beard, wondering if it were real or not, when he said, 'Your wife has told me a great deal about you.'

'Indeed? And what has she said?'

'She's very worried.'

'Why?'

'Because she says you have changed and she does not understand why.'

'It's she who has changed.'

The monk smiled. 'That's true. In the last few months Anna has experienced a genuine revolution in her life.'

'Then why should I not change as well?'

'There are many different kinds of change.'

'Why do you approve of hers and not mine?'

'Because she now has a new light in her eyes.'

A bell rang somewhere in the depths of the building. This was all beginning to get under my skin.

'The usual discredited clap-trap! "The eyes are the windows of the soul", etcetera, etcetera. We now have computers capable of quasi-human reasoning and you still believe that rubbish. Or, worse, you want me to believe it.'

He looked at me steadily with his dark eyes. I felt like some exotic animal in a cage. He was scrutinising me and I had no means of self-defence. He's had his chance, I thought. It's time to cut it short, speak plainly.

I rose brusquely to my feet, knocking over my chair in the process.

'Why don't you stop play-acting?' I shouted louder than I had intended.

The monk sat motionless, his expression unchanged, his eyes unblinking. 'Now I understand,' he said softly.

'Understand what?' I shouted.

I drove on the way back.

'Not a bad actor, your friend,' I said. 'Almost inspires respect. Almost.'

'At times I get the impression you've gone mad.'

'Then we're both mad. I'm Napoleon. Who are you?'

As I spoke I pressed the accelerator down angrily. I felt I had to stamp on something.

'Saverio, I know you think it's odd, but my life has changed. The change has come about by some invisible agency.'

'I don't believe in anything I can't see.'

'Yet you believe in the laws of chemistry.'

'Everything that exists is the result of chemistry. Chemistry and physics. Me, you, this car, petrol, the road surface, trees. That's what makes life what it is.'

'But who made them? Who made the laws that gave us life?'

'The laws have always existed.'

'Not true. God made the laws.'

'Of course. And man is descended from the apes and soon fire will rain upon the earth again. Am I right?'

'Don't laugh at me.'

'I'm not laughing at you. Do you still have the address of that psychologist you consulted when Giulia was born?'

'You talk like this because you're envious.'

'And what should I be envious about? Your fairy stories? No thanks. I believed in Father Christmas until I was six and that's enough.'

'I believe in God, not Father Christmas.'

'If Giulia died you'd stop believing.'

'We're in God's keeping whatever happens.'

'You reckon? Let's see,' I said, putting my foot down on the accelerator harder than before.

'Slow down!' shouted Anna. 'Think of our daughter!'

'We're in God's keeping aren't we? Let's see.'

So saying, I swerved at full speed on to the other side of the road. Seconds later we found ourselves in the path of an oncoming car. I wrenched the wheel round a fraction of a second before the impact. Back on our side of the road, I laughed nervously.

'So, who kept us safe? Who steered us out of trouble? God, or me?'

Anna wept, her face hidden in her hands, her body doubled up 'You're wicked,' she kept saying. 'You're a wicked man.'

I made a show of comforting her. 'Don't say that. I was only joking.'

Her tears brought joy to the very depths of my soul.

IV

The wood was now almost completely burnt. Only thirty or so trees still looked healthy. And you only had to look more closely to see that even these were showing the first signs of decay. I had been trying to solve the problem for nearly a year, but a solution still evaded me. After testing for moulds and various kinds of rot I had tried to pin the blame on various species of insect but had found no trace of any of them. Then I wondered about acid rain. I had seen whole pine forests destroyed by this near the Great Lakes in North America. There's too much heavy industry in the Po Valley, I reasoned, too many gases pumped into the air, and when the wind changes direction they become trapped in the surrounding valleys.

I had been pretty convinced by this theory, but an analysis of the water over the last few months had once again proved me wrong. The wood was dying and I could not understand why. The client wanted an answer and I kept fobbing him off. I was gathering material for a report; it was not yet finalised. The suspicion that there was a virus at work grew daily. But when you say virus you say something and nothing. Insects have their own laws; to fight them you only have to know how they think and find an enemy that will devour them. But the only law that a virus obeys is anarchy. It lives every-where, does as it likes and has its own set of rules. It lives but its objective is not the life of its host organism but its devastation, its death. It has not one face but many. Every time you succeed in identifying one, it changes its disguise and its password, slips over the border and has put itself out of reach yet again.

I spent whole days among those trees in their death throes. A dying tree is deeply disturbing. Especially to someone whose job it is to save it. A tree dies silently and its trunk remains standing for a long time, too long, like a finger pointing towards the sky. A finger that advertises your powerlessness. You knew all about its life-cycle yet in spite of that you could do nothing for it.

Thinking back over those days as I have during the last few years, I have often told myself that even the wood contributed in some way to the tragedy. There was a virus in the wood and another virus in my body. In contact with each other, they produced a deadly mixture.

Had I been looking after a flourishing garden at that time, everything might have been different. Coming to the garden with my mind full of dark thoughts, the stillness, the ordered loveliness of the garden would have dissipated them. In the big glasshouse the citrus trees would have been in flower and the borders ablaze with colour. Hearing the garden's song of beauty, life's shadows would have melted away.

Instead, I came every morning to a dying wood. I spent the whole day there with needles raining down upon me. I was losing control of my wife and losing control of the larches. It was, in simple truth, too much for a lone man.

Up there, I thought only of Anna and how to avenge myself. At home, on the other hand, I thought about the wood, about finding the best solution. One day or another, I would have set fire to it.

In bed, I ground my teeth so hard that one night Anna woke me up saying, 'Listen! There must be a mouse in the room . . .'

It must have been the third or fourth of May. Summer Time had started and I had stayed in the wood later than usual. By the time I got home it was well after nine o'clock. The windows were dark, there was no one in. I was tired, humiliated. I was looking forward to a hot meal, some sign of affection. After all, was it not for them that I worked myself to death every blessed day?

Suddenly, my fury exploded. I began to kick everything I could and throw things down from their shelves. I seized our wedding photograph and hurled it to the floor, breaking the frame and the glass, then I tore the photograph into confetti-sized pieces. When the door opened I scrunched them in the palm of my hand.

Anna looked tired.

'What a dreadful day!' she said. 'I got a puncture, and the spare wheel was punctured too.'

I went up to her and blew the pieces in her face. 'This', I said, 'is all that remains of our marriage.'

'Why do you say that?'

'Why?! Why?!' I began to shout. 'Why??? I slave for my family all day long and when I get home I'm a single man. I no longer have a wife or daughter. All the poor idiot's good for is to bring in the money. But the poor idiot has had it, had it up to here!'

Giulia took refuge behind her mother's legs.

'Calm down, Saverio, calm down. As I said, it was just one of those things.'

Like a coffee-pot left too long on the gas, I felt the pressure rising.

'And that's all you can say!' I shouted. And then I did something I would never have thought possible. I slapped her face.

There was a moment of complete silence. The phone rang but no one answered it. Giulia said, 'Naughty Papa.'

Anna picked her up and kissed her on the forehead.

'No, Papa isn't naughty. He's just very tired. Look, we'll stroke his face.'

Giulia hesitated with her little hand half-raised. There was surprise and fear in her eyes. So Anna guided her hand to my cheek.

'Dear Papa, dear Papa!'

Her touch was light and cool on my burning face.

'I hate you,' I hissed in Anna's ear as I strode out.

I had neither the car keys nor my wallet with me. To go back for them would have been too humiliating. Where else could I sleep that night if not in the cellar?

I now know with hindsight that the cellar was the last obstacle to be negotiated, the last marker to be circled before my journey's end. I could have walked down the road, dropped into the first bar I came across, got drunk and collapsed on to a bench in the park. I could have gone to a friend's house and talked like a madman until first light. I could have done many things, but instead, like an automaton, I began to climb down the steps.

In the cellar I found the last piece of the puzzle. A bicycle. A brand-new bicycle with a red bow tied to the bell. A carrier bag printed with the name of a menswear shop hung on the handlebar.

I had been right all along. There was a man mixed up in Anna's change, a man arrogant enough to hide his bike in my cellar. Indeed, it was better to come by bike than by car, it was not nearly as easy to trace. Why was it there? I wondered.

Perhaps he had been caught by the rain one day, so Anna had offered to drive him home. 'Leave your bike in the cellar,' she probably said, 'after all, my husband never sets foot in it.'

While I was driving myself mad over that wood, they

were in my bed, between my sheets, whispering sweet nothings.

Was it the consultant or not? For the moment this was of absolutely no importance to me. I knew all I needed to know, I knew I had not been mistaken.

Now the fire burning the larches blazed up in me. I felt the flames licking the trunk, the branches crackling just before crashing to the ground.

Sleep was impossible in such a place, so for a while I just sat there. Then I saw two old barbells. Picking them up I began to do some exercises. I exercised the pectoral muscles, the dorsals, then did some short bursts of running on the spot, some press-ups and then more work on the pectorals. I felt a tremendous energy inside me. The basis of all energy is some form of heat. To keep from exploding, I had to dissipate it. In the cellar I couldn't see when day dawned, so I had to keep checking my watch. It had a button that illuminated the face for a few moments.

Half past five.

Six o'clock.

A quarter past six.

At eight Anna took Giulia to her nursery school. I would wait until she got back and then go up and tell her what I thought about her conduct. That same morning I would go to the solicitor and ask for a separation. A separation blaming her and claiming custody of the child. I felt close to victory.

Everything happened very quickly. At half past eight I went upstairs. In front of the door to the flat there was a large white dog I had never seen before.

'Out of my way!' I said.

But it just sat there looking at me. So I seized it by the scruff of its neck and threw it down the stairs.

Anna had not yet returned. I stood by the door and waited for her. I waited for five or ten minutes.

When she came in and saw me she said, 'Where did you sleep? I've been worried sick all night.' She arranged her face into an expression of concern.

'Didn't you notice? I was very close.'

'Close? Where?'

'Right under your feet.'

'In the cellar?'

'In the cellar.'

I studied her expression and gloated. She looked disappointed. 'So you saw everything?'

'I saw everything.'

I expected her to start sobbing, to throw herself at my feet imploring forgiveness. But she smiled, even her eyes were merry. She opened her arms, saying, 'Well then, happy birth . . .'

Why was I still holding one of those barbells? I raised it and it came down on her forehead. There was a dull thud and Anna fell to the ground like a rag dropped on the floor.

V

I've heard no more about the wood. I wonder what happened to all my notes, all the folders with the analyses and test results. The landowner most probably abandoned all attempts to save it.

One morning two workmen would have arrived with a chainsaw and felled the trees one after the other. For a whole week the valley would have been full of the sound of death. Metal teeth attacking what was once living tissue. Then the noise would have ceased and the stream would have started to babble again. The woodpeckers would have found other trees to peck and the goldfinches and redpolls would have flown stupefied over the great bare patch that was once their world.

Losing teeth, losing hair. At night that was all I ever dreamt about. The wood dying and my losing all my teeth. Toothless and bald. The teeth didn't fall out one at a time, but all at once. As they hit the floor they rattled like glass marbles.

The way my hair went was no different. I passed my hand through it and whole clumps came away as if from a wig. So I wept. I wept quietly, silently. How could I go anywhere looking like this? With no teeth and no hair I would either be laughed at or pitied. I could inspire neither respect nor fear. So I no longer wanted to be seen in public.

The wood was dead and Anna was dead too. I saw her lying on the floor and felt impotent, as with the trees. I hadn't realised how easy it was to throw the switch. I had hardly touched her and she had gone.

For several minutes I thought she was play-acting and kept repeating, 'Come on, get up. I was only fooling.'

I fetched her a glass of cold water.

Her mouth remained shut and the water ran down her neck, wetting her blouse.

Could I have run away? I certainly had enough time. I could have taken the car and made for the border. I could have put her in a sack and dumped her in the river.

But I didn't. I sat beside her holding her hand.

When someone knocked on the door I went to open it.

It was the postman. I took the telegram from him and said, 'Come in. I've killed my wife.'

Giulia was still at the nursery school.

A month later, the solicitor showed me a daily paper with her photo in it. I knew it was her by the shoes, the pinny, the little lunch-basket. The face was covered by a fuzzy blob from which emerged two little pigtails tied with a bow of check ribbon. The photo must have been taken on the day of the tragedy because only Anna could tie bows like that. While I was washing I used to hear her singing, 'Whose are these two little pigtails? They belong to a little mouse.'

Someone I'd never seen before was holding her hand. She looked like a rag doll, her arms hanging limply, her feet dragging on the ground. Had they told her, or had she worked it out for herself? Concealing her face, however, was sheer hypocrisy. The caption under the photo read: *Little Alice (not her real name) daughter of the agronomist who murdered his wife.*

Then one day, when I was already here surrounded by the smell and the sound of the sea, the scales suddenly dropped from my eyes and I understood why the wood had died. It had been killed not by insects nor cankers nor viruses but simply by jealousy. Jealousy because larches grow surrounded by white firs, red firs and Scots pine. In summer they are so alike that laymen refer to them all as Christmas trees, but in winter everything is different. Larches shed their leaves while firs and pine trees keep their needles. So while they stand naked in the freezing cold, they see the others wrapped in a soft blanket of snow. Passers-by say, 'Look how pretty these are and how depressing the others, the dead ones.'

So the larches became jealous. Unable to come to

terms with it, they kept asking themselves: what have they got that we haven't? Why, if God made us, did he not make us equal? He gave all three needles and the same pyramid shape. We all grow at the same altitude and provide food for the same kinds of animals. Our wood is used for making good boxes. Our resin is distilled to cure bronchial illnesses. Then why should the pines and conifers be so favoured?

For the last couple of years I have been corresponding with Anna's friend the monk. He made the first move. I didn't reply immediately. On the contrary, when his letters began arriving I tore them up. 'What does he want from me?' I cried. 'Am I not suffering enough as it is?' Eventually I wrote to him, asking him to desist. He replied. I waited another few months and then I, too, replied. He is the only person who has been in touch with me all this time.

He was vastly amused at my theory accounting for the death of the wood. He did, however, add a comment. *The larches*, he wrote, *are jealous not of the perennial needles, but of love. Does the same not hold true for men? Why do you think that Cain killed Abel? Because he felt that his brother was loved more than himself. And why did Joseph's brothers throw him down the well? Because their father favoured him by giving him a long-sleeved tunic, the same tunic that was later found, bloodstained, in the sand.*

Those who love risk more than other people and often have to pay a very high price. In many years of spiritual counselling I have never ceased to marvel at this. Instead of opening the heart, love often closes it. Why? Perhaps we are frightened that, like food, water or money, it could be snatched away from us by someone more covetous than ourselves and devoured before our very eyes? But love is like the air. Infinite. It cannot be broken into little pieces, stuffed into a haversack or a handbag, kept in a larder. We cannot take just a portion of love because then we would always be finding someone whose portion seemed larger.

This is how the demon of jealousy devastates the world. The fear of not having enough makes us mean. Grasp, grasp. The more I grasp and grasp, the more frightened I am of losing, of not having got enough.

Do you recall our first meeting? The colour of your soul was fiery red. There was no wickedness in you, only confusion. Fires are caused by carelessness. We throw away a cigarette-end and that cigarette-end sets a whole forest ablaze.

You loved Anna and were afraid of losing her. That's what you always tell me. But have you ever asked yourself if you really loved her? Did you ever see Anna as a real person? Or was your love for her narcissistic? You loved her love for you, the way in which you were able to protect her. Did you love her vulnerability, her dependency? When she became a strong, an autonomous person, your feelings were turned on their head. You began to fear Anna from the moment she freed herself from fear. This is not a play on words, but a serious point on which you should reflect.

What is life when lived in constant fear? Such a life means keeping one's head constantly bowed. It is the life of a slave. But the destiny to which we are called is not that of slaves but that of sons and brothers. It is the destiny of love and liberty. Because true liberty does not mean doing whatever we like, but living without fear.

I often think of the last time I spoke to your wife. It was the night before the tragedy. Anna phoned me. I heard the note of anxiety in her voice.

'Saverio slapped my face and disappeared. He has never done anything like this before. The worst of it is that even our little girl has begun to be afraid of him.'

'He won't do anything rash?'

'I hope not. It's his birthday tomorrow,' she continued after a pause. 'I've bought him the bicycle he wanted. I do so hope he

will like it and calm down a little. Beyond that, I know we can't expect a marriage to be always plain sailing. Saverio lives in his own little cocoon and is frightened of being dragged out of it. There was a time when we were both living together in the cocoon, then I left it and he was on his own. He seemed to be shouting to me to go back inside.'

'And do you want to return?'

'Even if I wanted to, it would be impossible.' Then she added, 'Father, at last I've begun to understand those words from the Gospel . . .'

'Which ones?'

'About the world hating you. I had always wondered how it was possible for someone to hate you when you loved them so much.'

'Are you afraid?'

'I was, but not any longer. After all, patience is such a large part of love. I love my husband, I love our daughter. I know he loves us too, that it's only a question of time. All he has to do is leave behind his world of make-believe.'

You see, my dear Saverio, you have had the great privilege of touching rock bottom. I'm not being facetious. You can see things much more clearly from the lowest point than from any intermediate one. You could have bobbed up and down in a morass of confused feelings for the rest of your life. Things would have looked clearer sometimes and more opaque at others. You could have hated your wife in the morning and used emotional blackmail against her the same evening. There are couples who spend their whole lives without suspecting for one moment that there is a way out from the hell of their everyday life.

In your case, a grotesque kind of farce turned into tragedy. All you did was raise your hand in anger against Anna and three lives were destroyed. How long did it take? A second? Half a second? The next moment you were weeping beside the body of your wife.

Many people, at this point, would write the word 'finis'. I, by contrast, like to think that every end is in truth a new beginning. Certainly, something has ended, but 'something' is never everything. What we call the end is often only a kind of metamorphosis. You who know so much about insect life will have a very clear idea of what I mean. Anna is dead, but a part of Saverio is also dead. Now the living part of Saverio must get itself into gear again.

Self-pity, self-disgust, self-hate are all ways in which to negate the sacrifice of your wife. One day you will be judged by Another. Meanwhile, leave a space in your heart for compassion. Take up your haversack stuffed with blindness, violence, confusion, hate and bitterness, and begin to walk. Journey on even if others tell you it is useless or that you have forfeited the right. Journey on even if you can no longer see the road, even if you are enveloped in fog and find yourself treading warily along the edge of a precipice. And as you journey on, sooner or later you will notice that life is a route to be travelled, not a cocoon in which the most you can do is stretch your legs.

Most people do not really live but simply wait for life to end. What does life then become? Nothing but a series of diversions to keep boredom at bay. Then suddenly they are face to face with death or a devastating illness and they all cry, 'Swindle! Cheat! This was not in the rules of the game!'

But death is before us from the moment of our conception. Death stands there like an enigma, a perpetual question mark that we carry with us even in the happiest days of our lives.

If we are doomed to die, what sense is there in living? Every human being that is born must discover for him or herself the answer to this question. And discovery in this context does not mean mastering anything, but liberating ourselves. Liberating ourselves from all the baggage we carry in our haversacks, from greed, from envy, and above all from the idea of self.

I said 'liberation', but I could as well have said 'purification'. The purification of all that comes from our hearts, from our mouths, from that rarely mentioned but actually extraordinarily alive thing called 'sin'. Sin is not a transgression of the rules of some hierarchical order but a black veil we throw over ourselves. In that artificial blackout we see nothing, we feel nothing, yet are convinced that we understand everything.

So sin is a deficiency, an injury we do only to ourselves. Something that distances us dramatically from our true condition as creatures born to live in the Light. You had before you the luminous love of your wife, the trusting love of your child, and yet, in the thick veil that you had allowed to envelop you, not only could you not see them, but you mistook them for a threat.

The death of Anna must serve to rend that veil.

I am now advanced in years. In my long life I have seen and experienced many things, have had various visions of the world. With the passing of time, I have come to realise that these visions, apparently well founded and firmly established, were in reality like the refracting mirrors of a kaleidoscope. Every time I thought, now I've got it, this is the world, this is life, I must do this or that. How long did such ideas last? A puff of wind was enough to scatter them, and from the world created by the rearranged pieces another world emerged, and then another, and yet another.

At a certain point I rebelled. This, I cried, is folly. Existence is folly. I am folly. Everything in which I once believed is folly. For years I have prostrated myself before a void. For years I have spoken about a void. For years I have tried to persuade those close to me that the empty shell was full, that the fullness had a name and was worthy of veneration and respect. My despair was total. Every morning I rose and asked myself, what am I doing? Should I continue the life of a religious as if there were nothing wrong, spreading lies, or should I end my life here and now?

This was terrible, as you can imagine.

I heard confessions, received the confidences of souls that had lost their way, was expected to guide, to provide reassurance to all, while I myself was engulfed in total darkness and unable to confide my sense of disorientation to anyone. I turned the *kaleidoscope around and around furiously as I sought an answer to my questions. It was then, at that moment, that it slipped from my hands and fell, shattering into a thousand pieces. All at once I realised that everything I had believed in up to that moment was no more than a set of ideas, projections of my own anxieties and fears. I had wanted to grasp the ungraspable, impose limits upon it, give it a name, a time-limit. I had wanted to bring it into line with the limitations of my human understanding.*

That was when I truly started my own journey. The moment I found myself utterly naked, utterly defenceless, utterly dumb.

Nowadays I rise every morning, go to the window and know that this could be my last day. I no longer have any fear, nor sense of emptiness, but rather a trembling anticipation like that of an adolescent preparing for his first meeting with the Beloved.

Every morning just before dawn I stand at the window of this ugly concrete building and see the deserted fields and beyond them the dark silhouettes of farm buildings and factories and car headlights. What a lot of people are on their way to work at that hour! I stand there while the light gains the ascendancy over the dark.

The spectacle never ceases to amaze me. There is gentleness in that moment, and vulnerability and also immense potency. After a while, the black patch becomes a field of grass. I can see each separate blade and the dew clinging to it and the insects sipping the dew. I see sparrows sitting in the trees. I hear their cheeky, joyful chirruping and the more distinctive song of chaffinches and tits. I hear the noise of cars and see the people inside them. And, as clearly as I saw the dew on the blades of grass, I see their individual hearts, their histories, their cares, their worries. I see their hearts and the hearts of those close to them. Their children still asleep at home, snuggled in their warm beds, their wives already up and about and the old grandparents who have spent a sleepless night and are now listening to the radio. I see their hearts and hear them breathing. I hear the breaths of those coming into the world and the breaths of those leaving it, like a great concert played by the wind. It can sound like an organ or a flute. It rises and falls and rises again. It is a continuous two-way communication between heaven and earth.

And that is why every morning I lean my elbows on that ugly concrete windowsill and weep. I weep as perhaps only the very old can weep, softly, silently. I weep because I see love. The love that goes before us and the love that will gather us to itself. The love that, in spite of everything, accompanies us on every journey, even the shortest, the crookedest, the most sin-ridden. I weep for that love, and for all the hearts that are born, live and die as tightly sealed as coffins.

I pray for you. I pray that you one day may stand, like me, at your window.

Beneath the scrawled signature were a few more lines.

P.S. In the past few months I have met your daughter several times. She is a slender, long-limbed adolescent, wears her hair in a ponytail like her mother did and has her eyes, too, while her colouring and the shape of her hands are yours. She is a girl who thinks deeply and, like you, is accustomed to reason meticulously. It takes a while to become aware of the subtle uneasiness that broods deep inside her. The first couple of times we met she sheered brusquely away from the subject. The third time she managed to say, 'My father is a murderer.'

I responded with, 'Your father committed a dreadful, dreadful act, but he is not an evil man.'

We were sitting side by side on a low wall; she was wearing jeans frayed at the hem and she was swinging her legs nervously. Gazing into the distance, she said, 'No one kills unless they are evil.'

When we are adolescents we see everything in black and white! So I replied, 'At times people can do something bad because they are weak or confused, or frightened. What would you do, for instance, if a snake crawled out of this wall right now? Even if you love animals, you would probably kill it.'

After a while I was able to talk to her about the two of you, about the love that united her parents. 'When you were tiny, your mother was ill and your father stepped in and looked after you as few others would have done.'

A little plant of common mallow was growing at the foot of the wall. A bee, buzzing along, dived into it.

'You see,' I observed, 'the bee needs the flower. But the flower also needs the bee for its very existence. We are all connected by an invisible embrace. Your father needs you and you need your father.'

For a long time she said nothing, but sat there twisting a strand of hair this way and that. She kept her head turned away from me so that I couldn't see her face. She took two or three deep breaths, as if trying to fight against something that was suffocating her. Then, in a low, unsteady voice, she asked, 'But how about Mama, how would my mother feel about it?'

'Your mother', I said, 'would be the happiest mother in the world.'

Still clutching the letter I went to the window. It was dusk and the seagulls were returning from the mainland. There were two adult birds in the sky above me, gliding effortlessly on their great white wings. They were followed at a short distance by a younger one. He still had his darker juvenile plumage and was calling to them at regular intervals with a long piping cry.

The sea must have been rough for I could hear waves breaking against the rocks. Whenever this happened I heard my blood making the same whooshing sound as it was pumped from my heart to my ears and back to my heart again.

Tucked inside the monk's envelope was a second letter. It was smaller, written on pink squared paper.

Standing there I opened it while the sun sank below the horizon.

Dear Papa . . .

Susanna Tamaro

FOLLOW YOUR HEART

An international bestseller –
over three million copies sold worldwide

'Compulsively readable'
Elle

'One of the best novels of the '90s'
L'Avvenire

Winner of the Premio Donna Città di Roma 1994 and an international bestseller which has been translated into eighteen languages, *Follow Your Heart* is a profoundly moving and beautifully crafted meditation on existence.

With the wind whipping round the family house, an elderly Italian woman, driven by fear of her encroaching death, writes to her granddaughter in America. A love letter, a confession and above all a bequest for life, *Follow Your Heart* is a wise and beautiful novel, relevant to us all.

'The reasons for its success are immediately obvious. It has enormous charm and is packed with a philosophical wisdom we can immediately understand; it is narrated with a beguiling simplicity and intimacy so that the reader appears to have intruded upon a private correspondence. The series of love letters, explanations and confession gradually reveal a power and dignity which are both tender and evocative'
Glasgow Herald

VINTAGE